CANDLELIGHT
Ecstasy Supreme

"LISTEN TO ME. I LOVE YOU, AND I'M GOING TO LOVE YOU IN NEW YORK JUST AS MUCH AS I DO IN BOSTON."

"Oh, Tony, don't you see? You were a convict when I fell in love with you. We had our courtship in a prison waiting room! I'm a reminder . . . I'm a thread leading back to memories you're running to New York to get away from. You want a new life . . . a new identity."

He held her against him. "Come with me, Kate. You're the only part of the past I want to hold on to . . . the only part I need."

"I can't, Tony. I think what you're doing is a mistake. I don't believe in running away from the past. I believe in confronting ghosts, scaring the bloody daylights out of them, letting them know who's boss."

CANDLELIGHT ECSTASY SUPREMES

A QUESTION OF HONOR

Alison Tyler

A CANDLELIGHT ECSTASY SUPREME

Published by
Dell Publishing Co., Inc.
1 Dag Hammarskjold Plaza
New York, New York 10017

Dell ® TM 681510, Dell Publishing Co., Inc.

Candlelight Ecstasy Supreme is a trademark
of Dell Publishing Co., Inc.

Candlelight Ecstasy Romance®, 1,203,540, is a registered
trademark of Dell Publishing Co., Inc.

ISBN: 0-440-17189-X

Printed in the United States of America

First printing—March 1985

To Our Readers:

Candlelight Ecstasy is delighted to announce the start of a brand-new series—Ecstasy Supremes! Now you can enjoy a romance series unlike all the others—longer and more exciting, filled with more passion, adventure, and intrigue—the stories you've been waiting for.

In months to come we look forward to presenting books by many of your favorite authors and the very finest work from new authors of romantic fiction as well. As always, we are striving to present the unique, absorbing love stories that you enjoy most—the very best love has to offer.

Breathtaking and unforgettable, Ecstasy Supremes will follow in the great romantic tradition you've come to expect *only* from Candlelight Ecstasy.

Your suggestions and comments are always welcome. Please let us hear from you.

Sincerely,

The Editors
Candlelight Romances
1 Dag Hammarskjold Plaza
New York, New York 10017

PROLOGUE

A few lingering strains of a rock-'n'-roll song snapped off in mid note as the huge metal door clanked shut. Anthony Fielding imagined how the rest of the tune would go even though the song was unfamiliar to him. He had never cared for that kind of music and felt it was ironic that he'd probably be haunted for a long time by a melody he did not even like.

The corridor was an unrelenting gray, broken only by a somber brown desk near the metal-detector gate. Anthony Fielding had passed through those detectors dozens of times in airports around the world. But this endless gray passage, sealed at both ends, in no way resembled an airport.

The man behind the desk, dressed in a gray militarylike uniform, motioned him to come closer. Tony looked over his shoulder, a frown creasing his brow. The man shrugged, his expression bland. This was all in a day's work for him.

The man behind the desk nodded, mumbling a greeting to Tony's companion and scowling cynically at Tony. That's better, Tony thought. At least this guy fit his expectations, as lousy as they were.

"How's it going, Cooper?"

"Not too bad. Once I get our new buddy here settled in, I'm heading up to the Beale River for a little fishing." He handed the man behind the desk a thin manila folder and then flipped through the dozen keys on his large metal ring for the one that fit the cuffs.

Tony watched as he was released from the bracelet that had bound him to his companion for the last two hours. Only now did he discover his escort's name. Cooper, the other man had called him. That was the sum of what he had learned about his traveling partner. Not that he had tried to learn much. He had spent these last two hours in silence, and Cooper had seemed content to keep it that way. While he no doubt dreamed of trout and bass on the end of his fishing line, Anthony Fielding's mind remained numb. That was the way he wanted it to stay. The question was, could he manage it for twenty-four months? Eighteen, with good behavior.

Good behavior. That line always produced a grim smile on Tony Fielding's lips. Look where his good behavior had landed him so far.

"I hear the Beale's been low lately. You ought to try Hogan Pond. It's another thirty miles past Concord, but the trout are practically jumping out of the water to say hello. You should've seen the beauties I caught a couple of weeks ago."

Cooper grinned. "Yeah, well . . . the wife isn't too thrilled I'm going fishing at all. She's got her mother visiting. If I get back too late, I'll have the two of them jumping on me, and they won't be saying hello." They both had a laugh over that one. Tony remained silent, his expression blank. Their innocuous conversation seemed like yet another irony. Maybe he'd try Hogan Pond sometime, twenty-four months from now. Or eighteen —if he was lucky.

"Fielding?"

Tony directed his gaze toward the man behind the desk, who had called out his name. He almost shouted "Here" but caught himself. He was pretty sure that being flip would not count as "good behavior."

"Don't worry. It's not so bad inside. The trap is the worst part." His voice wasn't exactly sympathetic; more matter-of-fact.

So that's what they called this bleak, gray-on-gray corridor—the trap. Fitting name, he thought. A hollow cough overhead made him look up in surprise. A third man in gray peered down at him from a railing. Beside him was a rifle fit into a leather and metal holster. The man's hand was casually resting on the barrel, but Tony did not doubt for one moment that the guard would spring into action at the slightest provocation. Tony turned back to the man at the desk. He had no intention of provoking anyone.

He wished those flashes of old gangster films

would stop popping up in his mind. They seemed to be the only thoughts that pierced his general numbness. There were Cagney and Bogart, cigarette stubs between clenched teeth, organizing a break or cursing hotly at some guard as they got shoved into their cubicles. He had loved watching those films on TV when he was a kid. He'd even pretended to be—

"Walk on through," the man behind the desk ordered, nodding toward the metal detector.

Did they really think he could have picked up a "rod," or anything else for that matter, somewhere between the "trap" and the front room in which he'd been given a thorough body search? That was after relinquishing all of his possessions—a slim leather wallet, house keys, and a Swiss army knife he'd gotten from his father when he'd joined the boy scouts. He forgot the college ring he'd worn for the last twelve years. The guard reminded him about it. Tony had started to protest. Then he realized it could easily be stolen inside. He removed the ring and added it to the small pile. The guard slipped all his personal possessions into a small brown envelope. In bold lettering on the front he wrote Tony's name and then fit the envelope into a metal box already nearly full. So many identities locked inside, Tony thought as he watched the man carry the box to the vault.

The detector was silent as he walked through. His companion removed his key ring and laid it on the desk beside the cuffs before he followed Tony through the gate. He had no gun. It was too risky for the guards to carry weapons. Some hotshot prisoner could get hold of it. Anyway, it wasn't needed—not as long as the guy behind that railing, fifteen feet up, kept his hand on his trusty rifle.

"Okay, fellers, you're clear."

Tony was nudged again by Cooper. The man was in a hurry. Those fish were waiting to bite.

"I just might give Hogan Pond a try. The hell with the wife's nagging," Cooper said, giving the man behind the desk a broad grin. Tony glanced over at Cooper as they walked side by side down the gray passage to the end. Never had he envied anyone so much as he now envied this man, who had the freedom to choose to go fishing at Hogan Pond over the Beale River. A small privilege, but to Tony Fielding, who would be making few choices for quite a while, it seemed painfully precious.

The solid steel door slid open. The shock of daylight made Tony squint. He swayed slightly as the door banged shut behind him. That rock-'n'-roll melody drifted through his mind again as he headed down a path to the place he'd have to call home for the next two years. Or eighteen months . . . with good behavior.

CHAPTER ONE

The summer sun scorched the cracked pavement in the parking lot, making the narrow heels of Kate Stuart's pumps sink slightly into the softened asphalt. Tony Fielding had walked through the same parking lot almost twelve months earlier, on a day as hot as this one. Kate wasn't thinking about that as she strode briskly toward the two-story reception building, although she knew the exact date of his incarceration. She was too busy thinking about whether she was doing the right thing by coming to see him.

No. She was sure it was the right thing. What she wasn't sure of was how Anthony Fielding would feel about it. Switching the leather briefcase from her right hand to her left, she rubbed her moist palm against her gray linen skirt, then quickly looked down to make sure she hadn't left a mark.

The first thing she thought when she entered the cool lobby was that the place was nothing like what she had imagined. To her left was a long counter similar to those found in hotel lobbies.

Even the rows of cubbyholes against the wall were similar. Except these were much larger, holding purses and packages rather than notes.

Also in the manner of a hotel lobby, on the right was a small gift shop. Ignoring the sign on the wall that read CHECK IN with a thick black arrow pointing to the counter, Kate walked over to the display shelves. On close inspection she realized that everything there had been handmade by the prisoners. Tooled leather belts and wallets, scrimshaw cufflinks and earrings, wooden birdhouses, shell necklaces, and an assortment of other trinkets were laid out in a neat, orderly fashion, the name of the prisoner craftsman printed on a card beneath each object, along with the price.

Free enterprise behind locked doors. Kate found the idea ironic even though it pleased her. She glanced around for the name Fielding, but either he had chosen not to become an entrepreneur there or he'd sold out his wares.

A few other browsers wandered about, fingering some items, selecting a purchase or two. When they finished they either walked out, having had their visit, or else joined the others seated on green plastic chairs in the center of the room, waiting for their visit to begin.

Kate moved toward the check-in counter. A man in his fifties, dressed in a gray uniform, looked up from the sports page of his newspaper and told her to put her briefcase and pocketbook on the counter. He adjusted the dial of his transistor radio, trying to clear the static drowning out the Red Sox baseball game.

"You a lawyer?"

"No. I'm just visiting." Kate was irritated at her feeling of discomfort. She guardedly glanced over at the man who was rummaging through the sheets of paper in her briefcase. He seemed completely disinterested in her discomfort and in her presence. After he gave the inside and outside of her Italian leather case a thorough going-over, he shoved a form across to her.

"Fill it out," he ordered. "Print."

Kate printed in neat, even letters her name, address, phone number. Only when it came to the line asking her relationship to the inmate she was visiting did she hesitate. She had never even met Anthony Fielding. Still, she decided *friend* was the most innocuous of her choices. She noticed after she wrote it that it was printed much smaller than the other information.

"You need this case inside?"

"Um, yes. I have some papers I want to—"

He pushed it toward her, as disinterested in her explanation as everything else, once he'd felt certain that she wasn't smuggling in any contraband. He placed her pocketbook in a cubbyhole and handed her a metal number tag.

"Take a seat."

Kate hesitated. "This is the first time—"

"They'll call your name over the loudspeaker

14

after they track down the inmate. Takes ten, fifteen minutes."

Kate thanked him, but he was already buried in the sports page and didn't pay attention.

There were about twenty people scattered about the waiting room. Some sat alone, others in pairs. There were many more women than men, Kate noticed as she took a seat beside an older lady holding a carelessly opened gift-wrapped box. The woman was trying to fix it up as best she could. Kate gave her a sympathetic smile.

The woman shrugged. "It's for my son's birthday. A new shirt. White, naturally. Every year, a new white shirt. They tell you this is a progressive place with no uniforms. Street clothes allowed. As long as the shirt is white and the pants are black or navy blue." She smoothed out the shirt, placing the cover back on the box.

Kate took out a roll of Life Savers, offering one to the woman beside her and slipping one into her dry mouth. She was relieved that the place was air-conditioned. Tucking in a corner of her blouse, she wished she had chosen something other than a white one. Had she unconsciously dressed to fit the color scheme as well as the occasion?

More than twenty minutes went by before she heard her name called. She had begun to wonder if Anthony Fielding would agree to see her. Why should he? He didn't know a Kate Stuart, and he would never guess why she wanted to meet with him.

A guard at a gray metal door motioned to her as she stood up. She walked over.

"Stuart?"

She nodded.

He nodded in turn, his motion apparently a signal. The door slid open. Kate stepped into a long, gray tunnellike corridor. Another man motioned to her from behind a brown wooden desk.

The sharp contrast between the almost folksy atmosphere of the waiting room and this bleak, awesome passageway made Kate break out in a sweat, despite the fact that the area was almost chilly. For the first time she thought about what it must have been like for Anthony Fielding to hear the clanking slam of that metal door and know that it would not open again for a long, long time.

"You can put your briefcase on the desk, then take out all hairpins and barrettes, please." This man was young, under thirty, attractive, and showed more interest than the guard at the counter. He smiled pleasantly as Kate gave him a puzzled look.

"Sorry you've got to muss up your hairdo, but the detector will buzz like crazy if you walk through with all that metal in your pretty blond hair."

"Oh." She nodded dumbly.

"Once you step through, I'll give you a mirror so you can fix yourself up again." The man smiled more broadly, taking in her trim, shapely figure as well as the sophisticated coiffure.

Kate had the feeling he wasn't so obliging to all visitors. She began pulling out the pins in her hair, regretting having backed down on her decision to keep that appointment for a haircut a couple of weeks earlier. Instead she'd opted for an upsweep to get through the hot summer months.

She did not fail to notice the admiring glance from the guard as her hair cascaded in shimmering waves to her shoulders. She placed the handful of pins on the desk and walked through the gate. The buzzer went off, shrill and harsh in the sealed-off chamber.

She ran her fingers through her hair for an errant piece of metal, then remembered the thin gold bracelet on her slender wrist. She walked around the side of the gate so as not to trigger the alarm again and placed the bracelet beside the hairpins.

The guard smiled. "Anything else?"

She shook her head. Her breathing was shallow. She had never felt particularly claustrophobic before, but now she felt an urgent desire to get out of this unrelenting gray vault.

She breathed a sigh of relief when she walked through the silent detector. The guard, as he'd promised, handed her an oval mirror from his top desk drawer, but Kate was so eager to leave that she dropped the pins in her pocket, leaving her hair loose.

"I like it better that way," he said with a smile, handing her back the briefcase.

Kate ignored the compliment and headed down

the passageway. As she got within five feet of the end, a door, identical to the one at the beginning of the passage, noisily opened.

The light made her blink and she reached for her sunglasses, only to remember they had taken her purse from her in the waiting room. Squinting, she saw another guard walking toward her down a flower-edged path.

Kate viewed the well-kept green lawn and smatterings of colorful flower beds in front of the visiting center as one more incongruity. The officer led her inside the building.

She had expected rows of hard wooden seats facing one another, with a glass wall in between so that there could be no physical contact between the visitor and the prisoner. Instead she was shown into a fairly large lounge with a few upholstered couches and chairs and a dozen or so Early American–style maple benches padded with colorful cushions.

Nothing else was going according to her expectations, so she shouldn't have been surprised at Anthony Fielding's appearance when he was brought over to her bench by one of the guards. She had been sure she would at least recognize him. His file still contained his ID picture and vital statistics. Five feet eleven, sandy blond hair, blue eyes, weight 180. He was pleasant-looking in an Ivy League way with his crisp, neatly trimmed haircut, firm jawline, and well-shaped nose and lips. Only his eyes in the photograph, with their

18

intense gaze, belied the bland though attractive features. Kate found his eyes the most interesting aspect of Anthony Fielding.

It was finally his eyes that made her realize that it was Anthony Fielding in the flesh who looked down at her with a puzzled, slightly cautious expression. He was nothing like his picture. Either he didn't like the prison barber very much or he had decided the hell with regular haircuts. His hair was hung well below the top of the starched white collar of his shirt, and it was much lighter than the photo had shown. He sported a full beard and mustache, making his features seem sharper and more finely chiseled. He had also dropped a good twenty pounds, but his haphazardly rolled-up sleeves revealed muscular arms. There was, in fact, a tough, sinewy strength about the man.

Kate stood up and introduced herself, resting her briefcase against the seat. She started to extend her hand, but she could tell from the prisoner's expression that he was not going to extend his. She kept her hands at her sides, pressed slightly against her gray skirt to keep the trembling under control. She no longer worried about leaving marks on the material.

"I'm not quite sure how to begin, Mr. Fielding." Kate's voice was low, hesitant. His continued stare was not making it easier. "Can we sit down?" She sat, not waiting for his permission. She noticed his hesitation, but then he sat beside her, leaving a good couple of feet between them. He turned his gaze to her briefcase.

"I'm not a lawyer," she said with a smile that faded fast, as his expression remained unchanged.

"Now we both know what you're not." Anthony Fielding's voice was laced with a cynicism he made no effort to mask.

Kate looked at her hands, placed palms-down on the briefcase resting on her lap. When she lifted one hand, a dark impression of her fingers remained on the leather.

"It's very hot outside"—she turned to face him —"and I'm feeling very nervous. I've never been inside a prison before. It's not what I expected."

"Too bad I can't give you the grand tour."

"I work for Howell—"

Anthony Fielding leaped up. "So they decided to send someone over to help me celebrate my anniversary. How nice of you, Miss Stuart. And here I was, thinking everyone at the old place had forgotten about me. It's been a long time since anyone from Howell and Beck has paid a social call . . . or a business call. That's what this is, isn't it, Miss Stuart?"

"Please sit down and let me get a word in," she said, anger and embarrassment at his outburst tinging her cheeks red.

"Let me save us both some time. I'm not even going to bother demeaning myself any more by reiterating for the thousandth time that I'm innocent. See what twelve months in prison does for a

20

guy? Don't let the cheery flowers and lush green grass fool you, Miss Stuart. I assure you, medium security or not, this place is very much a prison. The proof is, when you storm angrily out of here, I cannot storm after you. Go back and tell your boss I still wouldn't say where the money is hidden. Period. Good-bye, Miss Stuart."

Kate caught hold of his sleeve. He gave her such a searing look that she almost backed off. His rage seemed barely held in check. She wanted to do what he suggested—storm out of the place and forget the whole thing. She was not the type to make waves, and here she was, creating a typhoon. She would not reverse the tide.

"Nobody sent me here, Mr. Fielding. In fact, if anyone from the company knew I had come— knew what I had brought with me—I'm pretty sure I'd be standing in the unemployment line next week. This whole thing may turn out to be a total waste of both our time." She paused, catching her breath, meeting his gaze head-on. "But it seems to me, to be perfectly honest, that you have more time to waste than I do." She stood up, briefcase in hand. "If you want me to leave, I will."

"Sit down, Miss Stuart." There was a bare hint of a smile on his lips. "You're right about one thing: I have plenty of time on my hands. And if nothing else, you're very easy on the eyes, so this won't be a complete waste. Besides, you've got me curious. That takes some doing lately." He sat down beside her, this time not as far away. "So what's in the briefcase that could cause you to lose your job? What exactly is your job there, anyway?"

"I'm the new chief accountant. Not really new. I've been with the company three months."

"Almost ready for a pension."

"Sometimes I feel like I am." She grinned, despite his sarcasm. "It's the best job I've ever had, but—"

"Forgive me if I can't concur. The particular pension they handed me wasn't the one I was expecting." He tapped the case.

Kate opened it and slid out a computer-generated transaction. She handed it to Anthony. He glanced at it and then shrugged. "This is it?"

"Do you notice anything unusual about the form?"

He looked again. "Until last year I must have seen hundreds of these orders. Mistaken double entry corrected so that the second figure is edited out. It happens all the time. Human error, Miss Stuart. It happens." His voice was again cynical, his irritation returning.

She took out several more sheets. "Take a look at these. I believe the usual method of correcting a double entry is to feed it through processing controls so that notification of the error goes out to the investor automatically. All seven of these were edited by computer, but no notification was sent." She paused, her hand trembling slightly. "That's not the part that worries me nearly as much as

22

seeing my initials on the bottom of several of the forms . . . forms I didn't sign."

Fielding took the other six forms from her and carefully studied all of them. Three others had her mark on them, indicating that the books had been corrected as well as the forms. He shook his head. "I gather you didn't sign any of these either."

"One of them is mine. The others are pretty good imitations. When I started picking up discrepancies on an occasional form, I figured someone else in the department had signed for me. But I couldn't track it down. Of course, the broker might have picked up his error before it was processed and simply signed the bottom line to save accounting some time. I've checked my records, and so far nothing wrong shows up. But I know that it's possible to bury figures that won't show until all the books have been gone through."

She handed Tony a final sheet. "This was the last one I found. I never would have gone over it so carefully if I hadn't started to get suspicious. I checked with the broker who made the error. He says he sent it down to processing like all the others and can't understand why I didn't get the pink copy at the same time." She looked from the sheet of paper to Tony. "I got it two days late . . . in a pile of already recorded accounts. It could have been a careless mistake. . . ."

"But you don't think so."

She shook her head. "If I hadn't been on my toes, these forms could have easily slid by me . . .

23

and when the books were gone over at the end of the fiscal quarter, I could have been held accountable for any loss that might have appeared. I could even have been accused of embezzling funds—just as you were." Her voice had gone painfully dry. She stuck her hand in her pocket and pulled out her Life Savers.

"How about a soda?" Tony offered.

"That would be great." She reached for her purse to get some change, then remembered her bag was resting in a cubicle in the waiting room.

"My treat. It's been a long time since I bought a girl a drink." Anthony Fielding stood up, reaching into his black chino pant pocket for some change and walked over to the soda machine. He returned with two cans and handed one to Kate.

She pulled the tab and took a long swallow. "Thanks." She waited until he set his can down. "So what do you think, Mr. Fielding?"

He smiled for the first time. "Tony."

"All right. Then call me Kate."

He nodded. "Maybe it's nothing, Kate. I know what you're thinking."

"It *is* similar, isn't it?"

"How much do you know about my case?"

"I don't know as much as I want to. Carl Isaacson was the broker whom I talked to about that corrected order form. He was kind of hostile at first. When he realized I wasn't trying to accuse him of doing anything underhanded, he softened a little. He talked quite a bit about you. He said that

24

the end-of-the-year audit picked up a series of manipulations on your transaction forms that could have allowed you to extract a hell of a lot of money from the company."

"Money they never actually proved I had in my possession."

"A large loss showed up in the reconciliation of what you had processed and what was actually recorded."

"Which means someone processed my transactions so that actual cash came out of certain accounts. I was the perfect candidate for the charge," Tony admitted. "The judge would have come down a lot harder on me if the prosecutor could have found a nice, juicy bank account in my name. As it is, I'm sure I'll have constant company when I finally leave here. They have to figure I'll dig up the money sometime." He gave her a hard, steady look. "Only they'll be wasting their time."

"That's why I came here. I realized after picking up these forms how easily I could be set up. It . . . it could have happened to you as well." She took the papers from Tony and placed them in her briefcase again. "I thought maybe we could help each other. If I knew more of the details of how this happened to you, it would help me keep my eye out for similar situations cropping up again. At least I'd know what to pay closer attention to. In the end, if something underhanded is really going on, I might come up with enough data to not only protect myself but possibly help you as well."

"Even if you do come up with anything—and I wouldn't say you had a hell of a lot of evidence to go on—how do you know someone isn't merely copying a method I tried first?"

"I don't know that," she admitted. "All I know is that you claimed you were set up and they never found that well-padded bank account; that, and the fact that these forms started popping up. Otherwise I wouldn't have paid attention. And so far I've managed to cover myself by making correction notations in my books. The amounts are certainly modest enough. But over the course of a year they could add up to quite a sum. Obviously some of them could very well be solely processing errors. But a few could slip by that aren't. A full reconciliation of accounts won't happen until February. By then, someone could have squirreled away a tidy nest egg . . . to go with the one he or she possibly hid away last year."

"By February I'll be out of this place. To be exact, on February seventh, I am a free man. Give or take three years of parole. All I want is to walk outside and forget this whole nightmare. Even if you manage to come up with hard evidence, which I'm not very optimistic about, it isn't going to help me particularly."

"That's not true. Okay, it might not get you out of prison sooner, but it could clear your name," she argued, astonished that her words seemed to make little impression.

He gave her a weary gaze. "Look, Kate, I understand you want to cover yourself. There's no one better than I who knows that setups could happen. I'll tell you some of the things to look out for, but I am not going to get caught up in exoneration fantasies again. For the first few months in here, all I dreamed about was clearing my name. It's what everyone in this rat hole dreams about . . . even the ones who are guilty."

"Now you don't care about that?"

"Do you have any idea what it's like to go through a trial, to stand before a judge and be told you are guilty as charged and sentenced . . ." His voice trailed off. "I want to forget this whole nightmare. I don't think I could go through a retrial, especially not after the fact. What if the judge decides the new evidence is inconclusive or circumstantial? All I get is a chance to relive an experience that nearly destroyed me in the first place. Look, I'm bitter and I'm angry. Sometimes the rage still wells up in me and I feel like putting my fist through the concrete wall of my cell. But I've learned during the past year that it isn't worth eating myself up alive over something I have no control over."

Kate faced him squarely. "If you were exonerated . . ."

"What? I could go back to being a happy-go-lucky investment broker, putting eighteen months of torture and grief behind me, pretending it was just a sad case of . . . human error. No, thanks. I've got a brother in Yonkers, New York, who owns a real estate company. He has a job waiting for me and has already written to the parole board, who will grant me permission to leave Massachusetts as long as I behave myself and visit a New York parole officer once a week."

"And live with the stigma of guilt. I don't understand you. I really don't. Okay, right now I don't have much to go on. But if I were to keep picking up little incongruities and started trying to do some more timely reconciliations, I might come up with enough evidence to matter."

Tony sighed. "Tell me something: If your phony signature stopped appearing on the bottoms of those forms, what would you do? You didn't show up today to try to prove some guy you never even heard of has been unjustly accused of a crime. You made this visit to save your own skin. That's okay; I can understand that. But don't march in, telling me you're going to rescue me from this lousy nightmare. Unless you're into lost causes as a hobby . . . ?"

Kate clutched her briefcase. "To say it wasn't easy to come here would be an understatement. And to sit here listening to you . . . feel sorry for yourself and . . . and be unwilling to show even a modicum of feeling about the fact that I could conceivably help you in the process of helping myself . . ." She pushed her hair angrily off her face.

"They made me take out all my pins," she muttered, deflated. "I'm sorry. I argued with myself for weeks before coming here. I was afraid I'd get your hopes up for nothing. And then another slightly odd transaction would pass through my hands. I read your file. There are quite a few people at the company who believe you are innocent and think you were set up. Only no one talks about it out loud. It took some prying on my part."

Her hand had been holding her hair back. She put it down. "I'm crazy for order." She smiled wistfully. "I guess that's why I chose accounting. A place for everything, everything in its place. At first I was just annoyed when I spotted a couple of those transactions. But then I began to feel uneasy about it.

"Sure, a big part of it was that my signature was on that bottom line. When I did some more prying, I found out that some of the evidence against you had to do with manipulated double entries processed similarly to these. It made me even more nervous. If you are innocent, as you say, then what if somebody's decided I'd make the next perfect mark? I knew I didn't have enough documentation collected to go to anyone in the company. Besides, whom could I trust? You don't work in a place three months and start throwing accusations around. Nothing shows up in the books . . . yet. I could be completely wrong."

She looked directly into his eyes. "I guess I wanted you to tell me I wasn't wrong. In a way, I didn't know who else I could talk to about all this. Once I really saw how possible it was for you to have been set up, I assumed you, of all people, would want to help me. And to answer your question, at this point, even if my name stopped appearing mysteriously on those forms, I wouldn't drop this. I have an obligation to the firm, and I don't intend to let someone start embezzling funds under my nose. Nor will I ignore the fact that you could be innocent and I may come up with the evidence to prove it," she said pointedly.

Tony studied her thoughtfully. "I guess escaping my pain has been the key to my success here. Now you show up and want to put an electric mixer to it. All my fantasies of revenge . . . of exoneration . . . of real freedom . . . are beginning to work their way back into my head. I can't say I'm pleased about that. But then, I'd have to be a total zombie not to be touched by your willingness to help me, even if it's to help yourself as well. It's been a long time. . . ." He smiled. "I notice I've been saying that a lot today. A year can be a collection of lonely, empty days. I've lost a career, a home, a girl I thought wanted to marry me one of these days . . ." His eyes dropped to his hands. "I haven't sat in this room with a beautiful woman for over ten months. I think that may be the only part of this visit I won't regret."

CHAPTER TWO

The radio was blaring another ball game. Red Sox ahead three runs. Kate walked directly over to the guard behind the counter. No hesitation this time. She was a pro. She placed her purse and briefcase on the counter, reaching for the check-in slip. She printed neatly; this time all the words were the same size. Relationship: Friend. Well, almost. She took her metal tag and her briefcase and sat down to wait for her name to be called. Fifteen, twenty minutes, she remembered.

Her name rang out over the loudspeaker in ten minutes. She smiled to herself before a flash of panic hit. That clanking, grinding metal door followed by that bleak gray tomb.

She wore a yellow dress today. No drab gray-and-white prison colors this time. Something soft and feminine, cool and delicate. It was a counterattack against this place, she had told herself when she slipped the silky dress over her head this morning. Or was she just fooling herself? Did she want Tony Fielding to throw out some more compliments? He'd said it had been over ten months since he'd been visited by an attractive woman.

And what about those first two months? Who had sat looking pretty and sexy then? His girl friend, of course. The one who was going to marry him one of these days . . . then changed her mind. That was an easy two plus two for Kate to total.

She wondered about the woman who'd jilted Tony Fielding when he was so completely defeated. She knew she didn't like her. What kind of woman couldn't wait eighteen months for the man she loved? She could have at least waited until he got out . . . given him a dream, if nothing else, to get him through these lonely, empty days. And then a thought flashed: The woman might believe that he was guilty. That could justify her decision not to wait for him. Kate might never learn the truth. So much was fantasy. She chastised herself when she started wondering if Tony had been doing any new fantasizing since she'd seen him two weeks before.

He was on her mind, especially at work. So many people knew him, and probably knew his almost bride-to-be. Kate wanted to ask questions, to find out more, even though she never asked herself directly why she wanted to know so much. But how could she casually walk up to someone and say, "Hey, you know that guy Fielding, who's rotting away in the clinker for stealing off with company moola? Well, I hear he had this lady love who walked out on him while he was down and out. Tell me about . . . the little bitch. How long were they together? How serious were they? Why'd she deal him such a low blow?"

Watch out, Katie, she warned herself. *You're feeling sorry for the guy and you're having fantasies about someone you don't even know. Someone who may be guilty, after all is said and done.* But she didn't believe it—that much she felt sure of after their first meeting. Too bad the judge and jury hadn't been so perceptive.

She stepped through the metal detector. Silence. She smiled again. The previous week she'd shopped in Bloomingdale's and bought two sets of plastic barrettes. With her hair swept up to keep her cool and collected, she felt less claustrophobic and clammy this time. But it still wasn't an easy path to walk. She doubted she could ever take it in her stride. Then the thought drifted by: Was she planning to come often enough to test it out?

A new guard sat behind the brown desk. He was a grim-looking man with a tight, straight line for a mouth and intimidating gray eyes that peered somewhere between her right eye and her ear. He fit the place to a T. She preferred him to the young guy from her last visit. Who needed to have a pass made at her in a bleak, gray tomb? She moved quickly down to the end of the passage.

This time she remembered to perch her sunglasses on top of her head. She was getting the hang of it. With perfect timing she dropped the

33

glasses over her eyes as the light hit her corneas. The same guard came out to greet her. She had an impulse to wave, breathe a little life into the mechanized scene, but she held herself in check. Instead she clutched her briefcase tighter, annoyed that her hand had started to sweat again.

There were only a few slips of paper inside. She didn't need the briefcase at all. She admitted to herself that she was using it for security, to support the fantasy that she had come today to present a lot more information and bits of evidence. She could have waited a few more weeks and possibly picked up something more substantial before returning to discuss anything further with Tony. So why had she decided to come back to this dismal place so soon?

That first meeting had left her shaken. The whole experience of the prison was part of it, but talking with Tony Fielding had been the real cause of her disturbed feelings. He had tried so hard to present a tough, strong exterior, but his vulnerability, his sadness, stood out as clearly as his rage. As clearly as his starched white shirt and well-pressed black chinos. He wasn't as grubby and disinterested in appearance as he was trying to make himself and others believe he was, shaggy hair and beard notwithstanding.

And his eyes—a disquieting shade of blue that altered with his mood, almost aquamarine one minute and then cool, pale turquoise the next. She had been drawn to his eyes even in that company photograph. In person they were more intense, more hypnotic. Maybe it was all that facial hair, she speculated, angry at her continued fantasies about the prisoner she thought she might be able to free. Stuff of which romances were made, she warned herself. The kind that got panned by critics and reviewers. Too unrealistic, too fanciful. Didn't she know it? She transferred the briefcase to her other hand and blew into her sweaty palm. She suddenly wished she hadn't worn this stupid dress. It was inappropriate, somehow teasing. She hadn't thought about that before. She'd just wanted to look good.

Tony was waiting in the lounge. He'd managed to secure one of the more comfortable sofas for the two of them. He waved her over, afraid to get up and lose the precious little comfort he could offer her. She waved back and strode toward him. He liked her walk: It was strong, efficient, yet feminine and graceful—like her. She hadn't said when she'd visit again. She hadn't even said for sure she would. Tony had ended their conversation without indicating whether or not he would help her to pursue the investigation. But somehow he knew she'd be back.

"That's a great dress," he said. "Haven't sat next to a beautiful girl in a gorgeous yellow dress in a long time." He grinned, then stopped. What was he doing, coming on so strong? He was going to be cool, pleasant, show her he was glad she'd come back, even apologize for his rude behavior last time. But he hadn't planned on practically drooling over her, nearly panting. *See what twelve months without a female body will do to you?* he scolded himself, crossing his legs when his body refused to listen.

Kate wanted to ask if the woman who jilted him had worn yellow the last time she visited, but instead she smiled and thanked him for the compliment. Was that a flush she saw hidden beneath that bushy dark-blond beard?

There was an awkward silence, Kate sitting primly with her briefcase on her lap again, Tony idly watching a young woman embrace her convict boyfriend over in the corner. Kate followed his glance.

"Do they allow that?"

"You get to have a kiss hello and a kiss good-bye, as long as you don't clinch for more than a couple of seconds. No necking in between, although it depends on who the guards are on duty and which cons are in favor at any particular time." He nodded toward the officer behind the desk. "Quinlan isn't too bad. As long as nothing really hot and heavy goes on, he looks the other way. A few of the others hold tight to the rules, some because they're sticklers for pure law and order, others because . . ." He let the sentence hang.

Kate changed the subject. "I've picked up several more odd transactions." She slipped them out of her briefcase. "It isn't much." The truth of that was only too self-evident. They both knew she hadn't come merely to present him with this measly documentation. "I don't know if someone is aware I'm getting suspicious or if—"

"I wanted to apologize for last time," Tony interrupted.

"No, don't be silly. You have nothing to apologize for. It was I. I should have written first, explained . . ."

They smiled shyly at each other.

"I haven't had many visitors lately," Tony said. "I have a sister in Duluth. She flew in twice. My brother comes up once every couple of months, but it's tough for him to get away from his business. And . . . being here together is hard on both of us. I think it almost hurts him more than it does me."

Kate had a strong desire to reach out to him, to touch him. It was a feeling of sympathy, but she kept her hands in her lap, poised over her briefcase, because she also felt a fluttering of something more, a feeling that had nothing to do with simple compassion. He *was* a very appealing man. What was so crazy about being attracted to him? He was also a prisoner—a con, as he called himself so harshly. Guilty or innocent, he was a man in jail, a man who was only allowed a hello and a good-bye kiss, and maybe a brief embrace in between if the guard looked the other way. She had no right to experience flashes of desire.

"Sorry, again," he muttered. "I promised myself, if you showed up, I wouldn't be morbid or hostile or act sorry for myself." He gave her a brief smile. "I'm afraid that's my basic repertoire these days."

"It's not hard to understand that," she said softly. "I wouldn't be dancing and cracking jokes in this place either. I'd probably come apart. How do you hold yourself together, Tony?" she asked, and then felt embarrassed at the frankness of her question.

"By saying over and over again in my head, 'Eighteen months with good behavior.' Then 'Seventeen . . . sixteen.' The old countdown. Must come from clicking off those sheep when I was trying to fall asleep as a kid. I'm down to six."

"Then five, four . . . I guess it must work." She cleared her throat.

"It has to. No choice. That's the toughest part." He shrugged. "Well, one of the toughest, not being able to have many choices. It's a big thrill at dinner each night getting a chance to decide whether I want the green beans or the peas. Little things mean a lot in here." He paused, his eyes drifting away. But not before Kate saw that they were a soft, clear blue. "It means a lot that you came back again. I find it easy to talk to you. Why is that?" He looked back at her now, his eyes creasing with gentle laugh lines at the corners.

"I'm the good-listener type," she said, smiling. "Quiet, pleasant . . . interested."

"You also feel sorry for me. I see it in those big hazel eyes of yours."

She didn't deny it. "Is that a crime?"

"Not the kind they put you behind bars for." His expression sobered.

She reached out for his hand, not worried about the meaning of the gesture. "I think you were dealt a bum rap. I've spoken with a friend of mine, a lawyer, about what has been going on. He thinks I have good reason to be suspicious. If I come up with some more hard data, I might be able to get a better lead on who is behind this thing. My lawyer believes that if someone is actually caught tampering with the books, you could easily get a new hearing."

Tony was silent, his eyes resting on her hand, placed so lightly on top of his. She removed it, putting it back in its proper place on her lap.

"I don't like the idea of you snooping. It could be dangerous." He shook his head slowly.

"I'm not going to confront anyone. All I'm going to do is try to track down any fictitious transactions or secret wire transfers and follow up more closely on how exceptions to the rule are accounted for. It's easy in my position. No one will even know I'm snooping."

"The guy who's cleverly covering his tracks will be clever enough to know if someone is trying to uncover them. You said yourself somebody may be getting nervous," he argued, certain she didn't really understand what she was getting herself into.

"I'm pretty clever myself," she insisted. "When I put my mind to something, I proceed with caution, but I finish what I begin."

"Is that one of your general rules?" he quipped.

"Absolutely." But her voice lacked authority. That question held some hidden meanings and they were both clever enough to uncover them.

Tony fished in his pocket for some change. "How about a soda?"

"Are you trying to change the subject?"

"Which one?" he asked pointedly.

Kate flushed. "I want to help you, Tony. Can I bring Chris Coleman with me next time? He's my lawyer friend. Maybe he can make you see that it's worth trying to get to the truth."

"How close a friend is he?" Before Kate could answer, he hurriedly apologized. "This isn't going to work. I'm not talking about unearthing a criminal now, Kate. Do you know what I mean?"

She looked up at him, nodding very slightly.

"You are beautiful, bright, warm. . . . Need I go on? I'm a con who hasn't had a woman . . ." He ran his tongue across his dry lips. "It's easy to fantasize in here. A sexy woman in a perfume commercial on TV is enough to set me off. I don't mean to be crass or vulgar, but you have a very direct effect on my body, Kate. It could get more than a little frustrating having these tête-à-têtes on a frequent basis. You see, I'm almost tempted to tell you to go ahead and investigate and keep me up-to-date each week on how it's going. But the truth is, it would only be a ploy to keep you visiting, even though there's a very real discomfort mingled with the pleasure."

Tony cleared his throat. "I'm telling you this now so you'll understand where I'm coming from right from the start. I've seen other cons in here creating fantasies out of thin air, because they need something to hold on to. Sometimes that countdown isn't enough. Sometimes I want someone so desperately to walk in here and throw her arms around me. . . . I want a guard to come over and tell me, 'Easy on those clinches, buddy.' I want to grab a quick feel of a warm, soft body so I have something real, tangible, to carry back to that cell with me." He caught his breath. "God, what's come over me? What am I saying to you? I must be going mad on top of everything else."

"I'm a good listener, remember? Easy to talk to." Her voice was soft, soothing. He shot her a glance, prepared to see pity in her eyes. But what he saw wasn't pity at all.

"Don't let me romanticize about this, Kate. And don't you. A prison visiting room isn't the real world. You don't belong here."

"Neither do you."

"Yeah, but you have a choice. I don't."

"Then let me choose, damn it! Stop deciding everything for me. As you said last week, I'm out to protect myself first and foremost. I'm going to pursue this thing whether you like it or not. But if you don't want to be involved in that, fine. I'd still like

41

to visit you again, unless you don't want me to come."

"Why do you want to visit?" he persisted.

"I don't know for sure yet," she answered honestly. "I'll keep you posted as I figure it out." She stood up. "See you next Saturday?" She waited.

"You'd better bring that friend of yours. We may need a chaperone." He stood beside her.

She grinned, then leaned over and kissed his cheek. When she walked out, he followed her with his eyes, his hand instinctively pressed against his face. He wondered how long he could hold on to the sensation.

Chris Coleman went through the small stack of papers a second time, jotting down notes on a lined yellow legal pad. Kate Stuart stood at the window, impatiently waiting for him to stop writing.

As soon as he set his pen down, she spoke. "I think we have quite a case at this point."

"Well . . . the beginnings anyway." Chris's voice was hesitant, with more bass than usual.

"What's the matter, Chris? A few weeks ago you sounded enthusiastic about this whole thing. Now I bring you more evidence, and instead of jumping on the case, you're pulling back."

"I never told you it was going to be a cinch, Kate. Yes, we've got some questionable transactions occurring, and some unusual processing of accounts. But there may be explanations for all of it that are completely on the up-and-up. Fielding was the first to admit that, nine out of ten times, these mistakes are human error and nothing more."

"Human error," she snapped. "God, I'm tired of those two words. You weren't using them before our meeting with Tony."

"Kate, the guy is walking a mighty thin tightrope in there. I've seen tougher men break under the pressure of prison. He's got a few more months and he can put it all behind him."

"He gave me that speech once before. I don't buy it. He's not going to put anything behind him, Chris. He's not that kind of man. Besides, Tony isn't my prime concern in all this. I'm out to protect my own neck, if you remember."

"Kate, do you think I don't see what's happening?" He walked over to the window. Standing beside her, he placed his hands lightly on her shoulders.

"What are you talking about?"

"Let me tell you something, honey. I've been in your shoes. Figuratively speaking, of course." He grinned. "I've worked on appeals cases with a couple of very attractive young women in jail. There is something poignantly romantic about a person wrongly imprisoned, especially a very good-looking person with a sensitive, gentle nature, fighting off rage, loneliness, heartbreak. It's easy to slip from feeling merely sympathetic to feeling . . ."

Kate walked away, Chris's hands dropping to

his sides. "You want to argue with me, but you can't," he went on. "Because you know there's a grain of truth in what I'm saying. And you know that Tony Fielding is very attracted to you as well."

"What's the big surprise in that? His fiancée walked out on him months ago . . . he's been away from women for a year . . . he's lonely, depressed, frustrated."

"Don't get me wrong, Kate. I think any guy would be a fool not to fall madly in love with you." He came up to her again, this time encircling her with his arms. "I haven't been locked away for a year and I'm still crazy about you. I guess the truth is, I'm feeling jealous."

"That's ridiculous, Chris. I'm not falling in love with . . . a total stranger. All right, I admit I do find Tony Fielding attractive. I enjoy talking with him. I . . . feel sorry for him. But that's it. That *and* wanting to help clear his name, because I know that he's innocent and I'm pretty sure I can prove it. Now, will you help or not?"

"This could be dangerous, Kate."

"Stop repeating every one of Tony's arguments, Chris."

"I can't help it. He's got several good ones. You wanted me to talk with him. I did. I also listened carefully to what he had to say. I don't want to see you getting hurt, Kate." He meant it in more ways than one. The tone in his voice made that clear.

"As soon as I have anything really substantial,

we'll know who at Howell and Beck we can trust. We'll take what we have to them and they can bring the FBI back in. They are the ones that can take all the true risks. No one need ever know anything until the culprit has been found."

Chris grinned. "You've been reading too many suspense stories."

Kate laughed. "Not true, Counselor. I don't particularly like that kind of book. Although maybe I ought to start reading them to pick up a few pointers."

"Never mind. Fact is a hell of a lot different than fiction, love. You just remember that and don't go snooping beyond what feels completely safe."

"I take that as a yes. You'll handle Tony's case."

"He hasn't said straight out he wants me to yet. But if he gives me the go-ahead, I'll do the best I can." He gave her a broad smile. "How can I resist you? Besides believing we probably do have something here, I have to protect my interests."

"Chris, give me a break. This is ground we've been over a few hundred times."

"You never know, Kate. Sometimes you take a guy for granted for a couple of years . . . think of him as a good friend, a pal . . . and then *wham,* one day you realize it's been true love all along."

Kate touched his cheek tenderly. "Now, why would I want to ruin a perfect friendship, not to mention the loss of the best lawyer in town? If we became lovers, in less than two months we'd both realize we'd made a drastic mistake, and then we'd mess everything up."

"Speak for yourself, honey. I think we'd make terrific lovers and it could last a lifetime."

"Let's settle for terrific friends . . . at least for now."

Chris shrugged. "One thing about being a lawyer: You learn to keep at a case until you've conclusively won or lost. And there's always the possibility of appeal." He gave her a tender kiss on the lips. "Say hello to Fielding for me the next time you visit."

Tony was particularly edgy this morning. He hadn't slept well in recent nights. Not that he'd really had what would be considered a good night's sleep since he'd walked into the prison. But that only made these past few nights even worse. His visit with Kate Stuart and Chris Coleman four days earlier was at the heart of his tension. This whole business was becoming more and more real. Coleman had shown guarded optimism about the chance of clearing his name, but it was positive nonetheless. And Kate, as usual, was brimming with determination and encouragement.

Her optimism was contagious. He was beginning to feel some hope, and it frightened him. She understood exactly how he felt. That frightened him, too . . . even more. He'd gone too long without warmth and empathy, too long without companionship and sex. Kate Stuart was taking up a prime spot in his fantasies, and Tony was smart enough to know that that's all they were. Still, the effect she had on him was disturbing. And he did not like discovering how dependent he was becoming on her visits.

She smiled when she saw he'd saved the couch again. Walking over, she presented him with a small package. Not surprisingly, it had been opened out front, but she had made a good attempt at repairing the damage.

"What's this? It isn't my birthday, is it? I haven't celebrated much in the way of holidays in here." He felt flustered, resting the package in his hand.

"It's not a holiday. I just wanted to bring you a little something. I noticed out in the waiting room that visitors were allowed to do that. I . . . I checked with the guard out front and he gave me a list of . . . of acceptable items." She focused on the package. "It wasn't a very long list."

"They don't like their prisoners coddled," he said with one of his cynical smiles, but then his expression softened.

"Well, go on and open it. I'm beginning to feel silly. It's no big deal."

Tony unwrapped the paper and lifted the lid of the box. Inside was a thin leather-bound book. He lifted it up, opening the cover to the first page. It was a book of poems by Robert Frost. He looked up from the book. "Thank you," he said softly.

"I thought reading poems might be a more

pleasant way to get through this time than counting days or sheep. Besides, you'd made a note in your résumé that you like poetry."

"Frost happens to be one of my favorites. He has a way of getting to the heart of things." He smiled self-consciously. "It was nice of you to think of me."

What could she say—that she thought of him often . . . more often than she cared to admit? Chris Coleman had something in common with Frost. He, too, had seen the heart of the matter. She should know better than to wear her heart on her sleeve. So why was she continuing to expose her feelings?

"I'm glad you like it," she said, hastily digging into her briefcase. "I've been making some notes I thought we should go over. There are some discrepancies I've highlighted, but you may have some better understanding of the various procedures. . . ."

He drew closer as she spread the papers across her lap. He tried to shift gears . . . to pay attention to the figures and words on the sheets . . . to ignore the delicate scent of her perfume and the attractive flush on her cheeks.

CHAPTER THREE

"You shaved."

"Disappointed?"

Kate shook her head as she unbuttoned her raincoat. She leaned over and kissed his cheek. "Mmmm." She smiled. "I like it."

Tony could feel that all-too-familiar pull in his gut. How many times had she come to see him now? As if he didn't know. Tony Fielding, the great timekeeper. Today would make it ten times. He knew the number of visits as well as he knew how long it had been since he'd felt those discomforting yet enticing flashes of desire, flashes that had been steadily turning into a constant. He helped her off with her raincoat. The proper host. He smiled pleasantly, giving no hint of the passion burning inside of him like a fuse.

Kate stole a glimpse of the newly clean-shaven man as he draped her wet coat over an empty wooden chair. She'd been taken aback at first. He looked so much more like that photograph in his file. Yet still different. It wasn't so much his features; it was what his face conveyed. A fascinating mixture of emotions that Kate felt she had barely begun to know and understand. Without the beard his feelings seemed closer to the surface, somehow more available.

There were always so many things left unsaid. Each time Kate sat in that waiting room, listening for her name to be called, she promised herself this time she would cut through the barriers Tony had erected. Her feelings for him grew with each visit. She wanted to talk about them. She believed in them. Just as she believed Tony felt something for her, despite his fiercely controlled behavior. He worked so hard at it. But then she'd catch his lingering gaze when he thought she was concentrating on something else. Or the few extra moments he took helping her on with her coat. When she kissed him good-bye—a friendly peck—he assiduously avoided her lips.

The guards had grown familiar with them. They seemed to have decided that the shy, awkward twosome had more going on between them than Kate or Tony could acknowledge. Most showed only a modicum of interest, but a few smiled when Tony and Kate kissed hello. One or two ribbed him: "Where'd you come by a dish like that, Fielding?" "Man, if she were my girl I'd kiss her like I meant it."

Kate guessed the remarks grew more graphic after she left. Tony seemed able to shuck them off, managing a comeback line that satisfied them. He always apologized to her afterward, guiding her toward the back of the room, away from the guards at the desk. Today was no different. At least, Kate didn't think it was.

"Hey, Fielding, you sure found yourself a gorgeous lady. It must be tough, old buddy," the guard at the desk said with a wink.

Kate could see Tony stiffen, his eyes narrowing. He was like a tiger about to pounce. She caught hold of his arm, feeling the muscles hard and tight.

"Come on, Tony. I'm used to their gibes; *you* certainly must be by now. What's wrong?"

He took a deep breath, forcing himself back under control. What was the matter with him? He looked over at Kate. They had to talk. Things were building up inside of him. He was losing the reins. And with only four more months to go, he had to get ahold of himself.

They walked to the rear of the room. It was a cold, rainy mid-September Saturday, and few people had come to visit. The room was almost empty. They took their usual seats on the blue sofa.

"You shouldn't have come today. It's miserable outside." His voice was low, severe.

"I wanted to see you," she said straightforwardly.

"You've found out something new?"

She smiled. "Tony, you know damn well by now that I haven't shown up here for these visits just about every Saturday afternoon only because of our investigation." She held her palms upward. "Look. No briefcase. I've come empty-handed.

Whoever is up to no good at Howell and Beck is either on vacation—probably a little trip around the world—or he's still hoping I'll stop snooping around so he can get on with his task."

"He . . . or she."

Kate grinned. "How chauvinistic of me. He . . . or she." She shifted in her seat, turning sideways to face him more directly. "Is that it? Are you beginning to get discouraged? I know something is going to break. I can feel it. Call it woman's intuition. Whatever it is, I sense it in the air at the office. Almost as though someone is watching, waiting to make his move. Sorry"—she smiled—"his or her move."

"I don't like it, Kate. Your intuition makes me like it even less. Listen to me: You aren't being used as a possible scapegoat anymore. You haven't come up with one other transaction form with your name forged on it. If someone is up to no good, it isn't your job to track down the culprit. And don't give me another speech about your responsibility to Howell and Beck."

"I wasn't going to," Kate said softly, looking carefully at Tony. "I'm not doing this for Howell and Beck. I'm not doing it only to protect myself either. I'm doing it because . . . I care about you, damn it. Don't you know that yet?"

"Kate . . ."

"And don't you start giving me any speeches about how easy it is to fantasize in here. I'm not fantasizing. You may not be in touch with your feelings, but I know when I care about somebody. Why do you have to make it so hard for both of us?"

"Am I?" he smiled.

"You are a tough nut to crack, Fielding."

"Why are you bothering? You're a gorgeous dish, just like the guard says. How come you're not snuggled up in some cozy little nook with the guy of your dreams? Somebody like Chris Coleman."

"Just what has Chris been telling you?"

"Ah, the discussions between a lawyer and his client are confidential," Tony said, trying for lightness but not quite managing it. "He didn't have to tell me anything. You only have to look at the guy when he so much as mentions your name to know how he feels about you."

"Chris and I are friends—good friends, but nothing more. He only thinks he'd like it to be different. Talk about fantasies; Chris has more than his share. He loves challenges. That's what makes him a great lawyer . . . and a poor choice for a lover. Don't take Chris too seriously, Tony. He has enough willing partners to keep him from pining too hard over me. It's been that way since I met him two years ago. I've seen Chris through quite a few romantic relationships since then."

"How many has he seen *you* through?" Tony looked at her closely, his features still strained.

Kate wished he would relax, let go just a little. "When I met Chris, I had recently broken up with a man. We'd been going together for quite a while.

53

When things didn't work out, I decided to concentrate on my career and let romance find its own way into my life. I was too busy to go looking. When I asked Chris to act as my lawyer, he was just starting a new love affair, which was a big help to our relationship. I hired him to handle an accident claim. Dumb thing . . . I slipped in the lobby of a movie theater: There was a tear in the carpet and my foot caught. A girl friend of mine introduced me to Chris. She was his femme fatale at the time. I think their affair lasted all of three months—probably a record for the illustrious Mr. Coleman. By staying friends, we've managed to go a lot longer. Plus, he's a terrific lawyer to have around in a pinch. Got me a very good settlement. Plus a few free passes to the theater," she teased, hoping to see a smile from Tony, but failing. "He's going to be as big a help to you." She reached for his hand.

"Who was the guy?"

"The guy?"

"The one who you were going with for quite a while."

"He was someone I met on a blind date, of all things. Nobody's supposed to have any luck with blind dates, right? Well, Jeff and I hit it off from the start. He was an architect. Very talented, but struggling to get a real break. He was with a small company that designed housing developments. It wasn't what Jeff wanted. He was just biding his time until something opened up. Well, his big break finally came. Unfortunately it came from California. The new job would give him the chance to work on some commercial projects—skyscrapers and the like—with a firm that was very well established. It was the proverbial chance of a lifetime. He took it, naturally."

"And he left you behind?"

Kate shrugged. "He bought two tickets to L.A. He was pretty sure I'd relent at the last minute and go along. I never did ask him if he was able to get a refund." She smiled. "For a few months I cursed myself plenty for not showing up at that airport. But later I felt I'd done what was best for me. Self-preservation first." She gave him a knowing look. "Then the rest can follow. I have a lot of ties in Boston. I love it here. And when Jeff got that job offer in L.A., I had just landed a pretty good job of my own. It was a situation in which neither of us wanted to give up what we had, so we ended giving up each other. Not right away: Jeff flew back east a few times. I made it out to L.A. exactly once. It was not my kind of town. Our affair went through a slow death, eased by our joint realization that what we'd had was good, but not something we couldn't live without."

She met Tony's steady gaze. "Now it's your turn."

"I'm not in Chris Coleman's league." Tony smiled.

"That's another point you have going for you."

She laughed, squeezing his hand. "I didn't take you for a roving Casanova."

"I haven't had too many opportunities these days," Tony said, his expression sullen again. What was the point of this whole dumb game? He knew Kate felt sorry for him and had let her feelings get carried away. He was a con. In four months he'd be a parolee. And three years after that, he'd be a man with an invisible yoke around his neck. Coleman might be the greatest lawyer since Clarence Darrow, but he couldn't create evidence out of thin air. Everything had dried up. Kate hadn't found one new clue to go on for weeks. His sexual fantasies were only tempered by the intermittent flashes of anger he couldn't help feeling toward her for getting his hopes up. That, coupled with his fears every time she did get close to anything, left him in a sweat of confusion and misery.

"You're avoiding the issue."

Tony stood up. "The issue is, you're wasting your time, Kate. You ought to be doing something better than sitting here with a con, playing true confessions," he said hotly. "I don't think you should keep coming here, Kate. In four months I'm out of this rat hole and on the first plane to New York. I'm leaving town just as sure as your ex-lover Jeff did. So there's no point to all this. You deserve a hell of a lot better. If you don't understand that, I do." He started toward the door leading back inside.

"There are all kinds of prisons, Tony." Her voice stopped him. He turned around, distraught at the look of hurt in her eyes, trying desperately to tell himself it was for the best.

She walked up to him. "That first day you told me if I got mad I could storm out of here and you couldn't follow me. Well, you have the same freedom of sorts. I can't chase you inside. I can't show up in that waiting room and demand that you see me. I can't force you to look beyond your circumstances to your feelings . . . or mine."

She touched his cheek, which was tender after shaving for the first time in a year. "There was something else that happened that day we met. I saw that you were a fighter—a reluctant fighter, a man who'd had the stuffing knocked clear out of him, not sure what he had left to fight with . . . or for. But you're certainly not a man who's given up. And you're not a man I'm willing to give up on."

She heard a weary breath, almost a moan, escape from Tony's lips. "Katie," he whispered, drawing her against him, searching out her lips, kissing her so deeply that he took her by surprise. She, too, moaned, her arms tightening around his neck. For several seconds they were both oblivious to their surroundings. Then a clapping sound filtered through, making them draw apart abruptly. The guard at the desk was giving them a rousing round of applause.

Kate caught the tightness in Tony's facial muscles. "It doesn't matter," she said softly.

"Yeah, a great place for necking," he spit out.

The jolt back to reality left them shaken, the rush of passion effectively masked. They both felt awkward, embarrassed. The difference was, Tony regretted what had happened; Kate most definitely didn't. For one thing, she had been yearning for that kiss. For another, it had kept Tony from fleeing, at least for the time being. She had no doubts there'd be other explosions before he was finally free of this awful place. It made her even more determined to unearth enough information to bring Tony's case up for appeal—and acquittal. Once that was accomplished, she felt the hard part would be over and the two of them would have a chance to allow their relationship to move forward.

The morning started out as usual. Kate arrived a few minutes before nine, drank her second cup of black coffee as she went through her in basket, made a few phone calls she hadn't gotten to on Wednesday afternoon, and held a ten-o'clock meeting with her two assistants.

"Kate, I thought you might want to take a look at this," Steve Geller said after the meeting was over. Steve was her chief assistant. He'd been with the company for nine months and was working toward his C.P.A. Kate didn't particularly like him. He made no bones about the fact that he didn't care for the idea of working under a woman, and as soon as he had that golden certificate, he planned to move out and up. But as grating as Steve could be, she had to admit that he was diligent and accurate—painstakingly so. She might feel a basic need for order, but Steve had taken that need and raised it to an obsession. His nit-picking about points that were of little importance was often irritating, not to mention time-consuming. Nevertheless, when he laid a computerized data sheet on her desk, she withheld her sigh of irritation, although she had too much work of her own to do to have to spend twenty minutes explaining to Steve how some minor computer error could be corrected in twenty seconds.

"What's the problem?"

Steve pointed to the third line. "Look at this double entry. Mitchell put through this same order yesterday. Either the order was voided after I picked up yesterday's sheets, or one of the programmers goofed and picked up the same information twice. I'll track it down, but what annoys me is that I picked up a similar double entry last week. By the time I checked on it, whoever made the boner covered their tracks."

Kate sat up sharply. "Which investor was it last week?"

"Peterson."

"I want to see all of the data sheets involved."

"Jeez, you're always on my back for bugging you about minor data errors. Now you're blowing

59

up because I'm taking care of it myself. You can't have it both ways," he snapped, then apologized: "Sorry, Kate. You'll see that I took care of it properly. I even had a talk with some of the computer operators and the two brokers who might have been at fault. Typical—everyone blamed the mistake on someone else. You want those reports this minute?" he asked, not sure whether he had appeased her. Her eyes were still flashing fire, but she did smile slightly as she nodded.

Want them that minute? She wanted them weeks ago. This could be *it*—the lead she'd been looking for. So the well hadn't dried up after all. The water was starting to flow again.

After Steve brought her the data sheets and pointed out the discrepancies—as if she wouldn't have been able to spot them herself—she locked her door, left word with her secretary to hold all calls for the next hour, and sat at her desk, intently going over both Mitchell's and Peterson's double entries. Then she realized what was missing: The original order sheet from which the computer operators worked. Did the errors lie in the original order or in the transfer of information on to the computer? She needed to get hold of those penciled sheets without arousing suspicion. There was no legitimate reason for her to have those papers. She would have to discreetly borrow them from the computer room. That meant waiting for a time when it was likely to be empty—lunchtime at the earliest. But some of the workers might bring in their lunch and stay put. The best time would be after work. Staying late was easy enough, since Kate often put in extra hours, finishing up her accounts. However, getting into the computer room was another story.

She wrote down the names Rob Peterson and Francia Mitchell. He . . . or she. Kate smiled to herself.

Those two names had both cropped up before. Not that they were the only two with a few more than average errors in their transaction sheets, but they were on the top of the list. Also, they had both had one particularly large double-entry error apiece. Kate lifted up her receiver and called down to the brokerage floor. She got Francia Mitchell on the line and asked her to come up to her office to go over a problem in one of Francia's transaction forms.

A few minutes later a slightly flustered Francia Mitchell was staring across the desk at Kate.

"I'm really embarrassed about this. It was a stupid mistake. I should know better than to put in an order without checking it over. You see, Bellmore and Sons phoned in for a new trust account on Thursday the twenty-first." She pointed to the original order. "Being the efficient soul I am, I immediately put the proceedings into the works. But I hadn't meant for them to get recorded until the next day. That Friday morning, when I processed the fifty thousand dollars, I discovered it was already on the day sheet. I'd put the date for deposit on my notes, but one of the programmers must not have picked it up. Good thing I checked; otherwise both entries could have gone through."

"If that second deposit went through to our bank," Kate mused aloud, "it would be possible for someone to take the money out of the account, along with a void on the books . . . say, through a wire transfer that might look perfectly legitimate until the account was reconciled with what actually came in."

"What are you saying?" Francia Mitchell said in a bare whisper.

"I'm saying something we both know is possible —theoretically, of course. I'm just making a plea for more caution, Miss Mitchell. If somebody mistakenly picked up that void and was able to break into the computer system, this company could be out some hard cash, based on your carelessness. Given the fact that Howell and Beck has already been burned once—the technique was slightly different, but close enough to worry me—it's my responsibility to make sure errors like this don't get by me."

"I'm an investor, Miss Stuart, not a computer whiz. I made an honest if stupid mistake. And the only transaction I put through was for a double-entry void, not an order for a wire transfer. That's certainly something you can check into."

"I always check into those things . . . as a matter of course."

Kate leaned back in her chair as Francia Mitchell stormed out of her office in a huff. *Well,* she thought to herself, *Peterson will be easier.* She'd had a little practice. She had set the ball in motion, realizing that if she didn't jump on this possible break, things would continue to move along at a snail's pace.

Kate did not check wire-transfer files as a matter of course, any more than she looked through investors' penciled orders. Fran Mitchell and Rob Peterson might or might not realize that. Either way, if one or both of them were involved in anything underhanded, the first thing they would do is try to get their hands on those transfer sheets. Only Kate had already sent for them from the computer room, and if either Mitchell or Peterson asked for those files, they would have to sign for them, which Kate longed to see. It would also be a coup to pick up a nice, neat phony wire transfer. Then she could lay the mess in Howell and Beck's laps and let them finish up the dirty work.

It was only slightly easier with Peterson. He was a lot more indignant and antagonistic. In the middle of his blowup, Todd Nichols, one of the clerks from the computer room, showed up with the file of wire-transfer sheets. Kate hastily took them from him at the door and stuck the sheets in her top file drawer. She was pretty sure Peterson couldn't see what they were from where he stood. She wasn't sorry to see him storm out.

It was close to lunchtime. Kate decided to grab a bite downstairs at the coffee shop before sitting down to work on those sheets. She carefully locked her files before leaving and then locked her office door, something she didn't bother to do if she was going to be away for only a short while. But she wasn't going to take any chances with what could be a gold mine of information sitting in that room.

Her tuna-fish sandwich was dry, the lone leaf of lettuce pathetically wilted; the plain white bread she'd ordered was toasted to a crisp dark brown. She left half of it over and washed down the few bites with a soda gone flat. If she were trying to diet, she couldn't have discovered a better place to eat. However, weight not being an issue, she bought a candy bar at the counter and ate it on her way back up to her office.

Her door was ajar. Kate hesitated before entering. It was still the middle of lunch hour and nobody was around. Nobody who should be, that was. Her eyes traveled down to the key hole. Someone had either gotten ahold of a key or was very adept at jimmying locks. There were no scratch marks. She swung the door wide open, making sure the room was empty before stepping inside and closing it behind her.

She knew immediately that somebody had been snooping around. Nothing was jarringly out of place, but Kate, with her passion for neatness, could spot the difference in the way the papers were laid out on her desk. And the drawers had definitely been gone through. Several sheets were in a different order. A box of paper clips had obviously fallen out while whoever it was had been riffling through her top drawer. The metal clips were dumped back into their box haphazardly.

Kate hurried over to the file cabinet. It was still locked. She leaned against the cold metal, sighing with relief. Then immediately she reached in her pocket for her key ring and unlocked the drawer. The papers were still there, thank God.

Well, she wanted some action and she was sure getting it. However, she hadn't reckoned on a direct frontal attack. She rang Chris Coleman up, too edgy to concentrate. She decided to bring the files over to his office and fill him in on what she'd already discovered. Then the two of them could go over the last week's wire transfers with a fine-tooth comb.

Chris's secretary told her that she expected him back within the hour. She checked his calendar, informing Kate on the phone he was free from two-thirty until four. Kate had her pencil in an appointment. That made her remember the penciled notations sitting in a file down in the computer room. It was still the lunch hour. If everyone was out . . . One break-in deserved another, she decided with a glint of determination in her eyes, now that the look of panic had evaporated. She also wanted to be sure neither Mitchell nor Peterson sought to retrieve their notes before she had a good, long look at them.

Kate thought she was in luck at first. Then, as

she stepped inside the computer room, she spied a blue uniform in the corner.

"Oh, you startled me. I . . . I was looking for . . . for Todd Nichols."

The messenger boy—really more a man than a boy—seemed as startled as she appeared. He tugged at the sleeve of his blue shirt, then stuck his hands in the pockets of his matching trousers. "Uh, he's due back from lunch any minute. Asked me to wait for him. Has some stuff for me to take over to Ormstead's."

Kate hesitated at the door. She probably could walk over to the files and find what she was looking for. This guy wouldn't have any idea what she was doing. But there was something about the way he watched her that made her uncomfortable. He was probably working up the courage to make a pass. She decided to come back when no one was around.

"I'll check in with Todd later. I've got to get to a meeting," she said, starting out of the room.

"You want to leave those files for him? I'll make sure he gets them."

Kate stared down for a moment at the file clutched under her arm. "No . . . I . . . I just wanted to talk with him about something. It can wait."

"You're in Accounting, right?" The messenger walked toward her.

"Yes. That's right."

"Yeah. I delivered some stuff to you a couple of times. You probably don't remember."

"I'm sorry. When I'm working, I'm sometimes oblivious to everything else going on around me."

"No big deal." He shrugged with a seductive smile. "Now you, you would be hard for any guy to forget."

Kate, anxious to leave before the man came on with a stronger pitch, nodded and made a fast exit.

She didn't realize until she stepped outside into the street that she had been perspiring. The cool breeze made her shiver.

CHAPTER FOUR

Chris Coleman's office was a few blocks from Kate's. She started walking down busy Boylston Street, her pace a bit quicker than normal. All the way over to Chris's place, she had the oddest sensation she was being followed. She told herself she was letting her imagination get carried away with this cloak-and-dagger business. Slowing down, she did turn once or twice just to ease her mind. Then, feeling foolish, she hurried on, checking her watch, noting that it was only a little after two. She hoped Chris would be back early.

Chris's secretary, Robin, was talking on the telephone when Kate walked into the plush maroon and gray office. Chris had very good taste—in his decorator and in the women who worked for him. Both his secretary and his legal assistant could have been models if they hadn't chosen to work for Chris.

Kate smiled at Robin, who was obviously trying to get off the line. She raised her perfectly shaped eyebrows and grimaced, saying several yesses into the mouthpiece. The door to Chris's office was open, and Kate could see that his room was empty.

Setting the file down beside her, she tried to decide between the *Vogue* and the *Forbes* resting on the side table. Chris breezed in before she made up her mind.

"Don't tell me the diligent Miss Stuart is playing hooky today," Chris teased, greeting her with a kiss as she stood up. "Perfect timing. I haven't had lunch yet. Come on, I'll buy you a steak."

Kate was still having trouble forgetting the awful tuna-fish sandwich. "No, thanks. And I'm not playing hooky. Have Robin call down for some food for you. We have work to do."

"Uh-oh," Chris said, studying her more closely. "This sounds serious."

Robin was still on the phone as Chris led Kate inside. He'd have to wait for his lunch. "Okay, shoot."

"Use another word, Counselor." Kate grinned. "I've had too much undercover adventure for one day."

As she filled Chris in on the details his sunny expression turned decidedly cloudy. Before he would even look at the file she'd brought with her, he leaned back in his chair, clearly ready to give her a lecture.

"I know, I know," Kate cut him off before he got the first word out. "I kind of set myself up."

" 'Kind of'? Kate, this isn't a little game you're playing. These folks don't play by the rules, honey.

You have put yourself right on the hot seat. If Mitchell or Peterson has been doctoring up the records, they're not going to just sit back and wait for you to gather up the evidence."

"I think the list goes beyond those two. I started counting as I walked over here. If one of the brokers isn't involved, then it could be anyone with direct access to the computers. There are a lot of clever people at Howell and Beck. Whoever set Tony up would have had to lay low for a while to avoid suspicion. Well, then I come along, new to the routine and green. So the embezzler figures, Why not give it a second go around. Only I'm not as green as he thinks. I start picking up these random, seemingly innocuous exceptions. His big mistake was pushing it one step too far. Once I spotted my initials on that first form I knew I had never signed, that was the beginning of the end for our friend."

"That's why I'm worried. This friend stands too much to lose. It's time to call in the big guns, Kate."

"But, Chris, right now it's all still circumstantial. If the FBI moves in too fast, they could mess up everything. I need to get ahold of those notes. They might hold the clue we need to actually point a finger."

"No, Kate. It's too dangerous. I'm not going to take any risks. . . ."

"Nothing really has happened, Chris. For all I know, the cleaning lady could have opened the door to my office and messed up my desk while she was dusting."

"Sure, sure. And the character you thought was following you?"

"Paranoia." She laughed. "Give it a week, Chris. I promise if I even get a hint of danger, I'll ring up the FBI quicker than you can say 'Kate, you're crazy.'"

"I'll wait until Monday, Kate—on the condition that you don't do anything else that will put you in the spotlight. The slightest—and I mean *slightest* —indication that you are in over your head . . . What am I saying? You're already diving into dangerous waters."

"Relax, Chris. Where's your sense of adventure?"

"How do you think Tony Fielding would react to your sense of adventure?" he threw back at her.

"I'm doing this for him. You and I both know Tony doesn't stand a chance in hell of an acquittal unless we get our hands on some cold, hard proof."

"You're really hooked on the guy," Chris said softly, digging his hands into the pockets of his gray wool slacks.

"I'm not sure. But I would like to get the opportunity to find out. Tony isn't much help. He retreats every time I take a step forward."

"He feels like a marked man, Kate. I'm not sure even an acquittal will eradicate those marks. Being in prison does lousy things to a person's head."

71

"Does he talk with you about it? I keep trying to get him to open up a little with me, but he holds everything inside. Sometimes I get so frustrated, I want to shake him."

"I know one thing: He's been pretty badly hurt by one woman who couldn't cope with the harsh, cruel facts. He isn't likely to set himself up for another beating."

"You mean his fiancée. Sweet Jennifer Simmons. Tony never talks about her. I found out her name at work."

"You wouldn't get much from him if he did discuss his breakup with you. You would have to read between the lines. The way he plays it, sweet Jen did the right thing to dump him. Why should she have to cope with that kind of stigma? He claims he was the one to drive her away."

"What do you want to bet he didn't have to work very hard?"

"I wouldn't bet a nickel. That's what I mean about reading between the lines. Tony has grown skilled at hiding his pain. He puts up all kinds of fronts. Even the bitterness is sometimes only camouflage. Inside, the man is hurting. He's also fighting against your trust, your feelings for him. At the same time they mean everything to him." Chris shrugged. "Damn it, why did I have to go and like the guy. He's stepped right in on me. Maybe getting our friend an acquittal will make this sizzling affair fizzle out. He might look less romantic without that sexy prison pallor," Chris said with a half-hearted smile.

"Get him out of there and we'll find out," Kate countered, giving him an affectionate squeeze on his shoulder.

"I'm doing my best."

"So am I."

On Friday morning Kate woke up with a splitting headache and a raspy throat. She put her hand to her forehead and immediately decided not to take her temperature; it would only depress her. She reset her alarm and went back to bed for another twenty minutes.

She felt no better when the buzzer went off a second time, but she forced herself to get up. Any other time she would have called in sick. But she knew Chris meant to keep to his ultimatum. On Monday morning he was planning to report all they had uncovered to the FBI. She wanted those penciled notes to be included in the file, and by Monday someone could alter or destroy them. It could already be too late, she realized. There was only one thing to do: Get her hands on them today.

A dose of aspirin didn't help her head, which hurt so much when she swallowed that she left her barely touched coffee in the kitchen sink and left for the office without being sure she was going to last the day. That meant making her move early. Given the need for haste, she decided to take the risk of somebody in the computer room finding out that she was borrowing those papers. If no one there was involved in the crime, she'd have nothing to worry about. She forced herself not to think about the alternative.

By ten o'clock she knew her fever was climbing. She could barely concentrate; numbers began to swim in front of her eyes. She needed to get home and climb into bed, which was exactly what she'd do—as soon as she made a brief stop in the computer room.

She was surprised to see the same messenger she'd walked in on the day before. He was having a cozy little conversation with Todd Nichols, and looked up sharply when she walked in. Then, immediately recognizing her, he gave her a provocative smile before he sauntered out.

Kate found the man offensive and irritating. When he left, she asked Todd about him.

"Don't pay any attention to Roy Maxwell. He's harmless. He likes to hang around here and pick up pointers about computers. He keeps telling me he plans to go to computer-programming school one day and doesn't want to start out a novice."

Helen Quinlan, one of the other programmers, piped in. "The guy's a born loser. It's a pity. He's got some smarts. But he's the type that's always talking big and never getting anywhere. Plus, he's crazy about the ponies. Maybe he's so interested in computers because he's trying to figure out a way to hit it big at the track. He obviously has had some luck with betting in the past: Last year he got himself a nifty little sports car. I saw him outside one day after work and he looked so proud of himself, I agreed to go for a quick spin around the block. Wouldn't you know, he came on heavy with the old standby lines. Since then I don't give him the time of day. Watch out for him—I recognized that sleazy gleam in his eye when he gave you the once-over."

Kate grinned. "I noticed it too. I'll remember not to go with him on any spins around the block." She turned back to Todd. "Listen, I'm coming down with a rotten cold and I'm going to take the rest of the day off. I wanted to take some work home with me." She paused for only the barest moment. "One of the brokers messed up a few times on his account sheet, and I thought I'd give him a hand . . . straighten out the mess. I wanted to run through his pencil notes on a few orders."

Todd gave her a puzzled look. "I don't think his notes would do you any good. All it shows is the same figures the printout sheet reads."

"Well, I just want to be sure."

"We're real careful down here, Miss Stuart. I guarantee you we copy number for number what the brokers put down."

Either Nichols's feelings were hurt or he was trying to keep her from those notes for other reasons. "I'm sure that's true, Todd, but I'd still like to borrow them. Unless there's any reason why I can't."

"Hey, suit yourself," he said coolly. "I was just trying to save you a little work."

Well, she'd made one enemy that day, but just then that was the least of her concerns. After Todd went to the files, extracted the notes, and handed them to her, Kate had the uncomfortable feeling that he, Helen, and the other two programmers in the room, who were busy at their computer terminals, all had their eyes on her back as she walked out of the room.

It was a relief to get back home. The first thing Kate did was take two more aspirin, along with a vitamin C tablet, and stretch out on the living-room couch with her newly acquired treasure. As she started sifting through the figures her eyes kept closing. After a short while she was fighting to stay awake. Finally her need for sleep won out. With the papers sprawled out on her lap, Kate leaned back against the cushions and closed her weary eyes, promising herself that she'd only take a fif-teen-minute catnap.

It was close to one o'clock when she dozed off. When she woke up it was after four. She might have slept through the rest of the afternoon if she hadn't been awakened by a scraping sound at her front door. For a moment she gazed in wonder at the doorknob as it slowly turned.

Then, as her adrenaline started to flow, she leaped off the couch and ran toward the door.

Thank God, she'd thought to put the safety chain on.

"Who's there?" Her voice was a high squeak, part fear, part the sore throat.

Abruptly the knob stopped turning. Kate leaned against the door, cupping her ear against the cold metal. She wished she had a peephole so she could see who was trying to pay an uninvited visit.

It could be a robbery attempt that had nothing to do with what was going on at work, but the coincidence seemed too unlikely. Most of the people at work had no idea she had taken the day off, so if anyone wanted to get their hands on the wire-transfer files she had taken, they might risk breaking into her apartment on the chance that she'd left the incriminating information at home—especially if they thought she was wise to somebody having already broken into her office to find them.

One thing made her feel a little better: She was narrowing down the suspects. The four people in the computer room all knew she was going straight home, so they wouldn't have tried to break in. She went back to thinking about Rob Peterson and Francia Mitchell. Then suddenly bits and pieces of her conversation with Helen Quinlan rushed into her head. She thought of what Helen had said about the messenger, Roy Maxwell, with his fancy new sports car and his penchant for betting on the horses. He was always hanging around the computer room, asking questions. Then Kate thought of her own reaction to him. Had she been looking in the wrong direction all along? Kate wasn't ready to abandon her other suspects, but Roy Maxwell moved way up on the list of possibilities.

She moved to the kitchen table and spread out the wire-transfer files, comparing them to the brokers' notes on the transactions. It was slow going, and by dinnertime she was only halfway through. She decided the best thing would be to fix herself a hot bowl of soup, get a good night's sleep, and finish in the morning with a fresh, clear mind. If things went according to her hopes, she might have some terrific news to give Tony on Saturday afternoon. She'd also make Chris happy by letting him call in the FBI sooner than she'd made him promise.

Every Saturday at one o'clock in the afternoon, Tony's spirits rose. He'd sit in his room (as a sign of its being a medium-security prison, the men lived behind locked doors instead of locked bars, thus the euphemism *room)* and wait for the guard to come by and tell him he had a visitor.

On this Saturday, one-thirty passed and still there was no rap on his door. Kate was never late. He chided himself for behaving like a mother hen. Why couldn't she be late? She hadn't taken a sacred vow to visit a con faithfully at one o'clock every damn Saturday afternoon.

He broke out in a cold sweat. The previous Saturday he'd blown up at her and told her to stop coming to see him. But then afterward, that kiss

. . . God, that kiss had knocked him for a loop. She'd melted against him, kissing him back just as he had fantasized a couple of thousand times. Only it was better than his fantasies. And worse. In his fantasies he was in control. He could make the endings turn out any way he wanted. And he knew exactly what he wanted. He could picture the two of them lying naked, their bodies entwined, making passionate love. It was a frustrating image, but images were all he had. So at least for the moment he could pretend. . . .

Where the hell was she? He couldn't believe she'd given up on him. She said she wouldn't, despite his stubborn refusal to let her get close. Didn't she know how much he wanted her? Didn't she know how terrified he was of dragging her into something she would later regret bitterly? He was back to stage one, resigned to his fate. He'd have to live with the burden of guilt for the rest of his life. He'd manage it. Hadn't he managed the past fourteen months of hell? It was his cross to bear, not Kate's.

Besides, he'd learned something important the last time they'd been together. Kate wasn't about to give up her job at Howell and Beck to go running off to New York with him. She hadn't gone off with that other guy, and they'd had a real relationship, a chance for the kind of intimacy Tony could only dream about with such a strong, determined lady.

By two-thirty he was imagining the worst. She'd

either decided to cut her losses or something terrible had happened to her. What if she'd finally uncovered something at work, something that could be dangerous? He'd warned her all along that her snooping could get her into serious trouble. And he knew how frustrated she was becoming. She was probably angry at herself for not being able to come up with more. Tony knew that she was sensitive to the fact that she might have built up his hopes for nothing. He'd been angry about that, but now he just wanted to know she was all right. Even if he never saw her again . . . No, he couldn't tolerate thinking that.

"Got a visitor, Fielding." The lock was unbolted and the door opened. Tony sprang out of the room as though he were on fire.

She was walking through the door, windblown, her face flushed, a wide smile on her lips. She rushed toward him, flinging her arms around him.

He was going to give her hell for causing him two hours of agony, but as soon as she pressed against him, he forgot everything but the joy of holding her. He tipped his head down to kiss her, but she turned away, pressing her cheek against his.

"I'm dying." She laughed. "You'd better not kiss me or you'll die with me. I'm probably moving from pneumonia to double pneumonia."

He pulled away from her, his eyes instantly registering concern. Then he pressed his lips against her forehead. "You have a fever. What are you doing here?"

"You've got to stop asking me that, Tony," she said with a grin. "Besides, today I would have dragged myself here if I'd broken both arms and legs and had whooping cough."

"You know, you had me half out of my mind, worrying about you."

Kate looked up at him, a warm smile still on her lips. "You should have faith in me, Tony. I told you I wouldn't give up on you."

He smiled back. "That was only my worry for the first hour or so. The rest of the time I had visions of you being kidnaped and held at gunpoint by a gang of embezzlers."

He noticed the subtle change in her features. "Something did happen to you." He gripped her by the shoulders.

"Nothing's happened. Take it easy." She hesitated before telling him about the break-in at her office and the attempted break-in at her home, but she figured he'd hear about it soon enough, and it was better if she was the one who told him. Anyway, the morning's homework had put everything in a new light. She finally had unearthed enough incriminating evidence to prove that somebody had definitely broken into the computer system and had been juggling the figures.

She took Tony's hand and led him to their usual seat. "Sit down and listen to me," she ordered. "I don't want you to say a word until I'm all through."

She started with her discovery. "I figured out exactly how the scheme is worked. A broker gets a call to open an account. Say John Doe wants to put in fifty thousand dollars. So the broker notes it down in pencil and then processes it through. Then the next day he gets the fifty thousand dollars in the mail. He goofs: forgets this is the same order he put through the day before and reenters it. Now John Doe is fifty thousand dollars richer than he started out. But of course the broker picks it up and hastily sends through a void."

"Kate, I know all this. Remember, I used to be a broker," he pointed out.

"Shhh. No interruptions. Where was I? Ah, yes. Now, all of this looks perfectly accurate on the books. John Doe started out with fifty thousand dollars and he ends up with fifty thousand dollars. No problem. Except"—and here Kate's hazel eyes started to sparkle—"if that extra fifty-thousand-dollar record happened to make its way into the company accounts figures. Somebody can then break into the system and wire-transfer out the erroneous funds." Kate told him about her visit to the computer room the day before and the subsequent near–break-in at her apartment. She kept her thoughts about Maxwell as a prime suspect to herself. It was still too soon to be throwing around accusations.

Tony blew up. "Do you realize what could have

happened? What if the creep didn't give a damn if you were home or not? He could have decided to take care of you along with a robbery. Don't you realize the risks you were taking? My God, Kate, what if something happened to you?"

She was glad she'd kept the office break-in to herself. Tony was upset enough.

"Nothing is going to happen to me. Now that the FBI will be in on this, whoever the guilty party is will have to realize I've turned everything over to them. You and Chris ought to get together: You make a great pair of worry warts." She reached out and took his hands. "Hey," she said softly, "don't you realize what this means? This news is your exit out of here. There's enough evidence now to prove you were set up, even if it takes awhile to track down the real culprit. I'm meeting Chris at my place as soon as I leave here. With what I've unearthed, he could have you out of here in days."

Tony was only slowly taking it all in. "I don't know, Kate. Maybe it's enough to reopen my case, but I don't want to get my hopes up too high. I know a lot of guys in here waiting for their retrials. It could take weeks, months. I might be out of here before anything is cleared up." He reached over and stroked her cheek. "Oh, Katie, you're a wonder. How did I ever luck out to find you?"

"I found you, remember?" she said softly.

"How could I forget? You haven't left my mind for more than a minute. I'm afraid I've walked right into something I warned us both against: I've let my fantasies run away with themselves. Got myself a clear case of prison romance."

"What do you intend to do about it?" She edged closer to him, ignoring all the other people in the room.

"I guess I'll do what the other cons do—grab hold of it while I can. The hell with tomorrow. Cons have to take one day at a time."

He put his arm around her, tilting her head up, bringing his lips to hers. His kiss sent a flurry of chills down her spine, and she responded fully, slipping her arms around his waist, crushing her breasts against his chest.

Tony felt a hand on his shoulder. "Lighten up, pal. We aren't in a movie balcony."

Kate flushed as Tony let go of her. She quickly looked up at him, afraid he'd explode at the guard. But he was smiling. The guard nodded, satisfied, and moved off.

He turned to Kate. "I have a much better imagination than that. A balcony seat in a movie theater is not what I have in mind for the two of us."

The sensual tone of his voice had as striking an effect on Kate as his touch did. She found herself growing warmer, certain that her and Tony's imaginations were moving along very similar lines.

"I'd better leave before our fantasies drive us *too* crazy," she whispered, then stood up, taking hold of his hand. "I am allowed a good-bye kiss, though, aren't I?"

He grinned. "I thought you didn't want to drive me crazy."

She put her arms around him, kissed him sweetly, and smiled. "I think we may be too far gone." She gave him a quick hug. "Chris is just going to have to work overtime and get you out of here fast."

Kate waved to Chris from across the street. He was standing in front of her apartment house, waiting for her. He waved back. Then as she stepped into the road she heard the roar of an engine mixed with Chris's loud yell. The sounds startled her so that she lost her balance and toppled back against the curb. Her fall probably saved her life.

A small sports car whizzed by her, missing her by the proverbial hairbreadth. Only it wasn't proverbial in this case. Chris was racing across the street to her. He was white with fear until he saw her get to her feet.

"My God, Kate. That crazy bastard could have killed you. I didn't even manage to get his license-plate number."

Kate was trembling so, she barely got the words out. "It doesn't matter. I recognized the driver."

CHAPTER FIVE

The case against Helen Quinlan, computer programmer employed at Howell and Beck for the past five years, did not move as quickly as Kate had expected. Kate had assumed that the programmer's arrest and indictment would lead rapidly to Tony's acquittal and release from prison. But she had sorely underestimated the slow arm of bureaucracy. Not that things didn't move quickly at first.

The day of the near hit-and-run, Jud Howell, senior head of Howell and Beck, met with a still somewhat shaken-up Kate, along with Chris and two FBI agents. Kate had recognized Helen Quinlan behind the wheel of that sports car. Helen Quinlan was picked up for questioning and a search warrant was issued shortly afterward, hopefully to uncover some evidence of the embezzling. The current year's company books were immediately confiscated, along with the previous year's accounts, after Chris presented enough just cause to reopen Tony's case.

Kate kept expecting Tony to get out any day,

but she should have known better. The roll of red tape turned out to be miles long. She was driving Chris Coleman crazy with her constant questions. Why couldn't he get some action? How long was it going to take? When would Tony's acquittal come up?

She was far more impatient than Tony. Even when she first broke the good news—omitting how close Helen's sports car had actually come—he seemed apprehensive. Oh, he was thrilled about the likelihood of the FBI discovering it was Quinlan who had doctored the books almost two years earlier, setting him up to take the rap. Finally he could see the end in sight. Yet, there was still an edge to his manner. Kate talked with Chris about it one day at lunch.

"It's natural, Kate. He's bound to be a little nervous about stepping out into the real world again." Chris gave her a reassuring smile. "You need to give the guy a chance to get used to the idea."

"Who's rushing him? I just don't understand why he isn't more excited. I mean, he's not only very likely to get released early, but he'll be leaving a free man, not a parolee, as he so frequently refers to himself. A free man, Chris! What is there to be so uptight about? Howell and Beck will certainly offer him his job back. My God, it's the least they can do. If I had my say, he'd be sitting up in one of the VP offices." She made a meager attempt at jabbing her fork into her chef's salad and then gave up, shoving her plate away.

Chris concentrated on his steak sandwich, knowing he had better keep his mouth shut. Unfortunately he underestimated Kate's powers of observation.

"Okay, Chris, spit it out. Something's on your mind." Kate attempted an encouraging smile. "Go on, I can take it." Her voice lacked conviction.

He looked up from his plate, propping his elbows up on the table. "Remind me never, never, again to be on the losing point of a triangle, honey. Or the monkey in the middle. I not only don't get the girl, but I end up being the one to carry all the bad news."

Kate unconsciously pulled her shoulders back and tilted her head higher. Stiff upper lip. Chris had to smile at her determined gesture. He reached across the table, taking her hand. "Tony's leaving town, Kate. He'd had me get started last month on his transfer papers. Yesterday, when I saw him and remarked how he wouldn't have to worry about parole anymore, he told me he still planned to head for New York. He'd written his brother the day before, telling him he definitely wanted to work in his real estate office."

"He doesn't have to go now." Her voice was a mixture of anger and confusion.

"Kate, I don't know what drives the man any more than you do. All I know is that he is determined to follow through with his plans."

"But we . . ." She left the sentence hanging. We what? Had a make-believe romance in a crazy unreal world? Not even that. A few kisses, a few brief hints. That's all they were—hints of something that might be. He was lonely, frustrated. He'd admitted that, admitted he longed for a dream to hold on to, a dream to get him through those dreary, endless days . . . and nights. Well, he wouldn't need fantasies much longer. In no time at all he'd be free to make his dreams a reality. Only it was obvious he wasn't planning to include her when he rejoined the real world.

"I have some other news," Chris said softly.

She gave him a blank look. He squeezed her hand. "Don't jump to too many conclusions, Kate. It's possible, if Howell and Beck makes a good enough offer, that Tony will reconsider his plans."

Kate shrugged. The issue went deeper than that. Howell and Beck wasn't the only investment company in town. If Tony wanted to stay in Boston to give the two of them a chance really to get to know each other, he could find someplace else to work. "What's the news?" she asked.

"I think we may get that acquittal sooner than I thought. Ben Hooper down at the FBI called. They've unearthed enough evidence to put our friend Miss Quinlan away for quite a while. When they started showing her the evidence, she began to sweat. At first she claimed she was only an accessory. She tried to implicate just about everyone at the company, including you. But the figures don't lie. Now Quinlan is crying about the fact that she got herself involved with a man a couple of years ago who had lots of big plans for the two of them. Only, of course, he lacked the cash to make their dreams come true. So Helen started playing around with the figures. She's a smart lady. She began real small. Then when she saw how easy it was—and probably how happy her boyfriend was at the little bonuses—she got greedy. Now that the FBI has enough to fry her and her boyfriend, she's singing a real long song, hoping to swing some kind of a deal. If she'd stopped last year, she probably would never have gotten caught. I bet she's regretting ever having chosen you as a possible patsy."

"I still can't believe it. I was becoming so sure it was that messenger guy, Maxwell. What a detective I am. The real criminal sits there, setting me up with a bunch of phony information about Maxwell—the new sports car, the gambling, hints about how he was always hanging around—and I put two and two together and come up with a big fat zero. What really threw me off was that attempted break-in to my apartment. Helen knew I was going home. Why would she try to get in and then run off when she heard my voice?"

"That was Helen's boyfriend, Mitchell, who wanted to pay a visit. Seems he and Helen had worked out the break-in the day before, when you took home the wire-transfer files. But when you surprised her by going home sick, she must not have been able to get in touch with Mitchell to tell him to nix the plan. And don't feel too bad about your powers of deduction: Helen was clever about a lot of things. Her story about Maxwell was pretty accurate. He did play the ponies, and he did hit it big last year and buy himself a new sports car. Of course, around that same time, Helen was buying her felonious lover a very nifty Triumph, which she borrowed the other day."

"I still can't believe she would really have tried to kill me."

"I don't think Helen knew what she was doing. She started to see the handwriting on the wall and panicked. Mitchell was one step ahead of her. The police picked him up at Logan Airport with a ticket for Mexico City in his pocket. He would have been perfectly happy to let his girl friend carry all the weight, just as he was happy to go through the thousands she stole for him. Turns out he liked to gamble even more than the messenger boy. Unfortunately for him and Helen, he wasn't very successful. Lost the booty as fast as she stole it—that's my guess."

"Chris, does this mean that Tony could get out any day now?"

He nodded, glad to see she was still interested in Tony. He didn't really believe she'd give up so easily.

"What are you going to do?" he asked as he watched her mental wheels start to turn.

"The first thing I'm going to do is have a little heart-to-heart with Mr. Howell. He's the partner

91

with the power . . . and, I hope, with a conscience."

Chris rubbed his nose. Kate recognized the action. It meant he was agitated and trying to think
of some way to offset it.

She smiled. It was now her turn to be reassuring. "You said yourself that Tony might feel differ-
ently if he knew Howell and Beck wanted to welcome him back with open arms." Her hands now
stretched across the table and covered his. "What
else can I do, Chris? We both know Tony's not his
most rational self right at this moment. I know
he's scared. But he can't just run off because of it
—not if I have any say in it. And I suddenly realize I have a hell of a lot to say, especially to Mr.
Tony Fielding."

"I don't get it, Tony. Are you trying to punish
them now, get back at them for not believing in
your innocence?" Kate threw up her hands in frustration. They'd been discussing this since she'd arrived at the prison twenty minutes before.

"For the hundredth time, Kate, that has nothing
to do with it." His tone was as frustrated as hers.

"And for the hundredth time, I don't believe
you. What more can the company do? Full restitu-
tion of salary, your old job back at more money, an
oral agreement to consider you for a promotion
within six months. My God, Tony, they're bending
over backward and all you want to do is kick them
in the butt."

Tony sighed. Maybe she was right. He had to admit his anger might have something to do with his decision.

She went for a more direct attack. "Is it that you don't want the job or . . . that you want to get away from *me?*" She couldn't hide the upset in her voice, but even if she could have, he would have read it in her eyes.

He stared at her. "New York isn't California."

"What does *that* mean?" she asked defensively.

"Kate, I have to get away from here for a while. There are too many reminders. . . . I can't walk around with a sign that says, 'Hey, folks, it was all a big mistake. I'm not an embezzler.' And in big bold letters on my back I can write *Acquitted.* Don't you see, Kate? I'd either have to constantly explain everything or suffer the looks, the whispers." His features turned angry. "Damn it, I've suffered enough. I'd have to be crazy to ask for more of it."

"What about us? Maybe you ought to put up another sign: 'Thanks a lot, Kate. I'll always be grateful.' " She turned her back, angry at herself for the tears that filled her eyes.

"I feel more than gratitude, Katie," he said softly, his hand lightly pressed against her back.

His touch disconcerted her, arousing feelings of anger and desire at the same time. "Do you?" was all she could get out.

"It's your feelings that concern me more than

93

mine. I don't want my suffering to rub off on you. I need some time. . . ."

"I thought you'd done enough time," she said bitingly.

"Don't, Kate. Don't turn this into a battle. As soon as the papers go through I'll be out of here. Chris says it'll be no more than two or three days. If it hadn't been for you, I'd be finishing out the rest of my sentence."

Kate gave him a glaring look.

"Okay, okay, so I am grateful; I'm not denying that. I'm also trying to tell you that I don't want to hurt you. An acquittal doesn't wipe out the books, Kate. Not where my feelings are concerned. I can't erase what's happened to me . . . or what it's done to me. I've been deprived of more than a year of my life. But worse than that, they also took away my self-esteem. I need to find some way to get it back."

"And you think you're going to find it in New York, away from me?"

"I don't know, Kate." He buried his face in his hands. "I can't think straight in this goddamn place."

She reached out and gently ran her fingers through his hair. "We'll talk once you're out, Tony."

He lifted his head, then drew her to him. He held her tightly, his lips pressed to her temple. There was so much he wanted to say to her, and so many reasons to keep silent. He had no idea what was waiting for him outside those concrete walls, no idea how he was going to cope with any of it. He kept thinking about how Kate would feel about him once he wasn't a cause célèbre.

And then there was Chris. He didn't agree with Kate's summation of Chris's feelings for her. Tony sensed they went deep. She was special. He knew it. Chris knew it. If he were out of the picture, he had no doubt that Chris would try to prove that to Kate. What claim did Tony have on her? Sure, just then she was caught up in an infatuation with a romantic hero. Outside those walls the hero would no longer exist. He'd be just a guy struggling with a stigma that no acquittal could erase.

"Thanks, Chris. I really appreciate this." Tony turned the collar of his raincoat up as he looked around. "Come on," he said abruptly, "let's get out of here."

Chris nodded, leading Tony to his car. They both got in. Neither said anything until they were a couple of blocks away.

"I'm not too happy about having lied to Kate," Chris said finally. "I don't think she's going to be too happy, either, when she finds out."

"You think I'm a coward, right?" He didn't wait for a reply. "I know it's crazy. Kate and I have been together . . ." He felt ridiculous tossing out the number of times. One day maybe he'd get out of the habit of counting. ". . . enough times. I guess the idea of seeing her outside, being free, scares me. I felt so damn nervous every time I thought of her waiting outside for me. I need a little time to get acclimated."

"Still heading for New York?"

Tony glanced at Chris. "I think it would be for the best."

Chris pursed his lips but didn't answer.

For a while they didn't speak, each absorbed by his own thoughts. Tony was the one who broke the silence. "Kate is a terrific girl."

Chris gave him a somber grin. "Yeah, don't we both know it."

Tony ignored the look and the tone in his voice. "You've both been—"

"Terrific, right?"

Now Tony laughed. "Right."

"I'm terrific, you're terrific, Kate's terrific . . . and we've got ourselves a very friendly little triangle."

"I'm stepping out of it," Tony said hesitantly.

Chris swung the car over to the curb and stopped it. "Let's get something straight, pal. I've been crazy about Kate Stuart for years now. She didn't give me the time of day in that department before you came along, and I can't say as how she's really likely to do it if you split. Not that I wouldn't keep trying; a free and clear field certainly wouldn't hurt. But don't go using me as a reason for skipping out of town. First of all, nobody's that altruistic. And second, you're not fooling me, and I think you're too smart to believe you're fooling yourself."

"Since you seem to understand so much, you tell me why I'm leaving," Tony countered defensively.

Chris gave him a long, hard look. "Believe it or not, love scares the hell out of me too. In my own way I've been on the lam for years."

"I had this New York plan set before I ever met Kate. I don't like the climate in Boston these days. There's too much of a chill in the air."

Chris shook his head. "I have a feeling Kate could be a big help in keeping the chill off."

"I don't think it would be fair to expect her to do that. It's my problem. Come on, Chris. This whole thing with Kate is based on fourteen damn sixty-minute visits to some con in prison she knows absolutely nothing about. I don't even know myself right now."

They pulled up in front of the Boston Sheraton, where Chris had booked a room for Tony. When Tony went to prison he had been forced to give up his apartment, because after paying his lawyers he was broke. His brother, Pete, had offered to carry it for him, but Pete had done enough. As it was, he had insisted on storing Tony's furniture and possessions for him.

Tony got out of the car as soon as Chris came to a stop, not waiting for the doorman to open the door. Bending down to the car window, he said, "Thanks again, Chris. I'll be in touch."

"Want me to come in with you? We could have a drink. . . ."

"No, I don't think a drink would do my stomach any good right now. Besides, I have some calls to make . . . my brother and sister, a couple of friends."

"Sure. I understand. Listen, if you need anything, you've got my number. Use it local or long distance."

"I will."

Tony stood on the curb, watching Chris's car pull out of the driveway. Chris lifted his hand in a final wave, but he didn't turn around to see Tony wave back.

The opulence of the lobby was in such sharp contrast to the environment Tony had spent the last year in, he felt his first real wave of culture shock. He smiled to himself. This kind of culture shock he could cope with. He was acutely aware not only of the appearance of the place but of the sounds, the fragrant smell of the flowers and plants, the vast assortment of clothes people wore, and most of all the freedom of movement.

No guards, no restrictions, nobody breathing down his neck every time he reached out for Kate. He felt such a strong desire for her at that moment that he could feel himself almost double up. He wanted to hold her so badly, it hurt. He really was a coward. He didn't need Chris's confirmation. He was afraid the whole thing between them wouldn't exist in the real world. He was so afraid to trust his feelings . . . or Kate's. He was a free man, and yet, he still felt locked up inside, confused, angry, hurt.

Tony was stretched out on top of the covers of his queen-size bed. He was still dressed and trying to decide between room service and going down to the coffee shop for dinner. He felt oddly uncomfortable about going downstairs and eating alone at a table with white linen napkins, choosing anything he liked from the menu. *Choices.* Tony smiled to himself, remembering the day he had talked with Kate about the meager choices a prisoner was allowed.

He had thought of calling her a dozen times. He kept putting it off. He called his sister, then his brother. Those were easy calls—happy, uncomplicated, full of love. He told his brother that he had made a reservation for a flight to New York the day after next. He'd give himself a day to do some shopping and tie up loose ends. He was going to have to call Kate before he got on that plane.

He reached for the telephone. Dialing room service, he ordered a ham sandwich and a glass of milk. When he hung up, he shook his head, smiling. One of the favorite topics in prison was what a guy would eat his first day out on the streets. Filet mignon vied with pizza for first place. A few guys had more exotic tastes, and then there were those whose fondest dream was a table full of Big Macs and fries. If his pals back in the can knew he'd settled for a ham sandwich and milk, they would have booted him out of their food fantasy club.

Twenty minutes later, when he heard the rap on the door, he called out to the waiter to come in.

Only it wasn't room service with his bland ham sandwich.

"I'm not sure what one is supposed to say to a man released from prison. Welcome home? Congratulations? Bon voyage?" Kate stood in the doorway, her eyes fixed on Tony.

He got up off the bed, feeling as if he were moving in slow motion: It felt like an eternity before he reached her, took her hand, and closed the door behind her. He saw the anger in her eyes, the hurt, the tension. But he also saw the desire. Just as he bent to kiss her, there was another knock on the door. They both jumped, startled by the sound. And he'd thought there would be no one to stop him from reaching out for her!

The waiter handed over the tray and took the tip that had been hastily extracted from Tony's pocket.

Kate gave the food a disapproving glance. "I guess it's a step above plain bread and water."

"I . . . I wasn't too hungry." He moved away.

She nodded. For a moment she looked as though she might turn and walk out. Then her eyes met his again across the distance he had created.

"Why, Tony? Why didn't you tell me you were getting out today? Don't you think I at least deserved that much?"

"Kate, I—"

"What were you going to do? Send me a post-card from New York? Or maybe a thank-you note with lots of flowery sentiment? All those months—did they really mean nothing more to you than that?" Her voice was disconsolate. She wasn't sure if she wanted to walk over to him and punch him in the nose or break down and cry her heart out.

"Katie," he said huskily, frozen to the spot. "I want you so badly, I'm going out of my mind."

"Then don't just stand there," she whispered, her heartbeat pounding in her ears, her body beginning to shiver.

He couldn't seem to move from the spot, a wave of panic sweeping over his passion. It had been so long since he'd made love to a woman. Now, wanting to so desperately, he was afraid he might fail.

And then she whispered his name softly, sensually. He moved toward her slowly as she stood waiting for him. Gently he wrapped her in his arms. For several moments they did nothing more. As his grasp tightened around her she nestled against him, her lips pressed close to his neck.

He felt shy and slightly clumsy as his hands began to caress her, tentatively at first and then with increasing force, so that he was thrown from a fear of being inadequate to the fear of physically hurting her because his need was so powerful. He caught himself and pulled away from her.

He gave her a wistful smile. "I'm out of practice."

Her hands went to the top button of his shirt and she began undoing each one. "Let me refresh your memory," she whispered breathlessly, as she was at last able to touch the flesh she had wanted to touch for so long. She ran her fingers over his chest, then slipped her hands around his waist to his back. Her lips brushed against his nipples, tiny kisses planted for eternity.

She removed his shirt. He fumbled with the zipper of her dress. She reached back to help him, their fingers entwining. He smiled down at her. "Thanks."

She tilted her head up, her golden hair tickling her bare back, her lips parted, inviting. So inviting. He felt possessed again, his urgent need skyrocketing. "Katie, Katie," he whispered, gazing down at her beautiful face before he descended on her lips. Forgetting all of his fears, he began kissing her with a ferocity matched by Kate's own burning desire. Deeply, voraciously, they kept kissing each other, holding, touching.

He slipped her dress off, his lips never leaving hers. His clumsiness vanished, his memory of other times no longer important. This was a first time, a time born of instinct and understanding—a time born of a passion that had begun as a tender, fragile flicker of light, that now burst into rainbow-colored flames.

His hands cupped her breasts, round, pink-tipped, the perfect size for him; the feel of her soft, firm flesh was beyond belief. No fantasy came close to the reality of the touch, the taste, the feel of her against him.

It was Kate who led the way to the bed. He would have devoured her standing right in the middle of the room. She slipped out of the rest of her clothes, then undressed him, tossing his things on the floor. She felt as if she were floating on a cloud, euphoric at the freedom she and Tony had both been granted. She loved the sense of abandon she felt. She had never felt she was a passionate woman. Too tidy, organized, in control. In the past those traits had come through even in her love-making. But that had been in the past. . . .

Maybe it was all the months of being denied something she wanted so very much. Maybe it was because tonight it felt so natural, so right. Whatever the reason, Kate let down all the barriers and inhibitions that had previously prevented her from really opening up. It was Tony who was shy, unsure of himself. Kate took his hands, guiding them to the places that sent her reeling with arousal; fondling him in ways that came not from any vast experience but from instinct and a curiosity she was unafraid to express.

Her tongue trailed a warm, moist line down the center of his chest. Tony cried out as she moved down lower. He felt as though he would burst. He tried to stop her, afraid he could not control the need that was tearing at him, but she shrugged him off, intent on the pleasure she knew he was feeling.

And then his body went into a spasm of trembling, a low, drawn-out moan on his lips. "Oh, God, Katie," he murmured as his breath returned. He pulled her up against him, his hands sliding up and down her back. Over and over he repeated her name and then he began kissing her again, the passion that had exploded only moments earlier returning with a force that stunned him.

He gently pushed her onto her back. First he kissed her lips again, then her eyes, her chin, the tender hollow of her throat. He sniffed the heady scent of her perfume—the one she always wore—but tonight it was more intoxicating. He loved the warm, heavy fullness of her breasts, his lips savoring the hardness of her nipples, his hands stroking the warm, satin-soft skin.

He took full advantage of what she had taught him about herself, adding to the knowledge his own discoveries, awakening new discoveries in Kate. She writhed and quivered beneath him as he lay between her thighs. She reached up for him, but he caught her hands, pinning them down against the sheets, a sultry smile on his lips. "You're so beautiful, Katie. Every inch of you, perfection. Let me show you how perfect."

She lay back, her arms sprawled outward as she willingly yielded to his possession of her body. There was no hesitation in the touch of his hands or his lips as he explored every part of her, caressing, kneading, taking tiny erotic bites that drove her to distraction.

He loved the low, throaty sound of his name on

her lips, mingled with soft, hungry moans as he carried her with him to a fever pitch of desire. When he pushed inside her, they both gasped at the sensation, a sensation they craved more than anything in the world at that moment. Their bodies moved as one, the rhythm slow, insistent, then wilder, more chaotic, as their excitement mounted toward the peak of climax.

Afterward his hand moved up and down her body with long, languorous strokes. Kate lay in his arms, her head on his chest, her fingers toying with the wisps of hair at the back of his neck. He hugged her tightly as she lifted her head to plant a warm, moist kiss on his lips.

"Oh, Katie, you are really something."

She smiled. "Did I ever tell you you are the only man who has ever called me Katie? I've been called Kate, Katherine, even Kathy, but never Katie. It sounds so nice."

"I'm glad I'm the first." He grinned. "*Katie* belongs to me, then."

Her expression grew serious. "She will . . . if you stick around. You do want to?"

He brushed her hair from her face, looking deeply into those warm hazel eyes. "I want to, Katie. I want to . . . with all my heart."

CHAPTER SIX

Kate rang the downstairs buzzer, using her special signal. Tony buzzed back and she stepped inside the warm mahogany-paneled lobby. There was a nice, cozy feeling about this small apartment building on Beacon Hill. Kate had been the one to find the apartment for Tony. She had heard about it and shown up with Tony first thing the next morning to beat out the other eager beavers. Tony had liked it, although his enthusiasm about the apartment did not match hers. Not that it ever seemed to.

The strain did not let up during the first month that Tony was out of prison. He had a great apartment, a terrific job, a woman who was crazy about him . . . and Kate felt as if she were walking around on eggshells. *How long does the period of adjustment last?* she wondered. Sure, she knew that Tony's reentry into Howell and Beck had its awkward moments. People felt embarrassed, uneasy about relating to him. They tried so hard to act natural that they came off stiff or glad-handed him to death. Tony wasn't much better. He had settled back into the routine of the job, but he was having as much trouble interacting with the rest of the staff as they were having with him.

That day, at lunch, when she had convinced Tony to join a few of the others, he had been particularly aloof, participating in the conversation only when Kate prodded him. She had made up her mind on her way over to his apartment for dinner that she'd confront Tony about his rude, hostile behavior. He seemed to be hampering his flow back into the mainstream every step of the way.

Now, when he greeted her at the door, his smile was warm, his embrace loving, tender.

"Mmmm, I missed you," he whispered in her ear, then nibbled her earlobe.

"We've only been apart for a few hours." Kate grinned. When he was like this, affectionate, playful, she could almost forget the other side of his nature.

"I made us a dinner tonight that's beyond belief. You are not to lift a finger. This one is all mine." He unbuttoned her coat and slipped his arms inside and around her waist for another hug before he slid the coat off her shoulders. He hung it up, put his arm around her, and led her to the living room. Champagne was chilling in a bucket, and several candles were lit in the otherwise darkened room. He swept her into his arms for a passionate kiss. "Maybe I ought to let the dinner burn," he teased, brushing her hair off to the side and kissing her neck.

Kate had a sneaking suspicion he had guessed that she was going to confront him about his behavior and was trying his hardest to avoid it. It was a good strategy. When everything was going so wonderfully for them, she really didn't want to ruin it.

He poured champagne and they toasted each other. Kate took a few sips, and Tony finished his. "Back to the coal mines," he said, putting down his glass.

"Can I help?" she asked.

"Nope. Why don't you put on some music, and then I want you to just sit there and look beautiful." He went into the kitchen and called out, "I never would have believed I'd turn out to be a halfway decent chef."

Kate heard a small crash.

"Or at least I will be . . . with some more practice. Don't worry. We haven't lost anything vital to the meal." He stuck his head out of the door. "You don't really like broccoli, do you?"

Kate grinned. "Not after it's hit the floor, anyway. Are you sure you don't want me—"

"I've got everything under control. First course in exactly two minutes."

Kate walked over to the table that was set for two in the corner of the living room. She rearranged the flowers that Tony must have picked up on his way home that evening. They hadn't been there the night before.

She'd been spending three, four nights a week with Tony. Either she'd come here or he'd go to her place. The nights were great—when Kate avoided any discussion of the day. She and Tony played house: She'd cook him dinner; sometimes they'd cook together or bring in Chinese food or submarine sandwiches. After dinner they'd watch something on TV or read, or they'd take a long walk when it wasn't too cold. They were quiet, relaxed evenings, a sense of contentment and peace suffusing both of them.

Kate did not press Tony about going out. Several times people at work invited them to a party or suggested a movie, but Tony was always quick to get out of it. When friends rang him at home, he would do the same. If Kate questioned him at all about it, his pat answer was that he loved having the time alone with her. It was a chance for them to talk, to get closer.

But Kate did most of the talking. She told Tony about what it was like growing up in rural New Hampshire, her friends at school, her first job. Tony listened attentively, clearly interested in learning more about her. But whenever she touched upon "current events," he withdrew into his cocoon.

Only when Kate pushed did Tony talk about himself. He opened up a little and told her about his childhood in the Midwest. His parents had both died by the time he was seventeen, and his older brother, Pete, had taken over looking after him, working to put him through college. Tony had been a bit of a goof-off in high school, but after his folks were gone and Pete was scraping together every cent he could to pay for tuition, Tony became serious about school. He worked while he attended college, so that between him and Pete, he was able to graduate with a degree in economics. The first two years he worked, he was able to pay Pete back every cent—not that Pete expected it. But Tony had been adamant. He explained to her that he always paid back his debts. She tried not to relate it to her situation and brushed aside the fear that Tony felt obligated to her and was just "paying back his debt" by being kind.

Her doubts vanished when they made love. Tony was a passionate yet tender lover. He was as intent on giving her pleasure as he was on fulfilling his own needs and desires. And the added edge of hunger, of making up for all of those frustrating months they'd both had to bear, gave their lovemaking a special heightened intensity and excitement.

"Soup's on." Tony carried two steaming bowls to the table and held out a chair for her.

"Looks good," she said, taking a deep whiff. "Spinach?"

"Close: asparagus."

Kate was duly complimentary. Tony really had gone all out. The soup was excellent, and the roast

110

leg of lamb that came next was done to tender pink perfection. Tony had even remembered the mint jelly.

"Quite a feast," Kate said, finishing her last savory bite of meat.

"It's kind of a celebration."

"Oh?"

"One whole month of freedom. Seems to me that's something to celebrate."

Kate smiled. "It certainly is." She hesitated a moment before continuing. "How . . . how does it feel?"

"Are you mad, woman?" he replied, laughing, not actually answering her question.

Kate proceeded with caution. "You were mighty determined to head for New York last month."

Tony caught hold of her hand and pulled her to him, settling her on his lap. He nuzzled her neck. "That was before I knew what I'd be missing."

She tilted her head back and looked directly at him. "You . . . you don't seem very happy at work. Are you sorry you went back to Howell and Beck?"

Tony didn't answer. Kate could feel his body tense.

"I realize everyone's a little uncomfortable around you," she said. "They're working so hard at treating you with kid gloves that it makes it worse. But *you* aren't exactly making it easy for them."

"Is that supposed to be part of my job too—

making everybody comfortable around Tony Fielding, the guy whom half of them believed was an embezzler and deserved those fourteen lousy months in jail? Oh, sure, everybody wants to be my pal now." His tone had turned bitter and harsh.

Kate stood up and started clearing off the table, determined not to get caught up in a screaming match, which is what she saw the discussion becoming. But Tony, usually as eager to avoid arguments as she, was already too worked up to back off.

He forcefully took the dishes out of her hands and put them back on the table. "Where the hell were all these pals of mine when I sat rotting away in that stinking jail? Answer me that, Kate. No, never mind. I'll tell you where they were: staying as far away as possible. Probably afraid Jud Howell or old Beck would think they were somehow involved, or that they would be viewed as guilty by association. I was the plague. Now the diagnosis has been changed, and everybody wants to pretend they were standing by my side all along."

Kate sighed. "Okay, they let you down. They didn't all believe in you the way you expected. I admit some of the people at work are first-class hypocrites, but others have been real friends. You told me yourself a few stayed in touch, even if they didn't visit in person. It isn't easy to get yourself to walk into that prison. Nobody knows that better than I do."

Tony didn't answer. He could feel the bitterness and anger biting at the back of his throat. The strain at work had been building up since his first day back. He hated the awkward greetings, the overly solicitous offers of help. They made him feel embarrassed, ashamed. . . .

He remembered once getting sick in school when he was a kid. Without warning he had retched right in the middle of his classroom. Everyone had shrieked, running away. The teacher wasn't too thrilled, either, but she got the janitor to clean up the mess and ordered everyone back to their seats. Tony went down to the nurse's office, and his mother picked him up and brought him home. He was crying—not because of how sick he felt, but because he was mortified that he had thrown up in front of his whole class. His mother said he was foolish to feel that way. Still, the next day at school was awful. Nobody teased him, but there was a dreadful awkwardness. . . .

It was like that now; this time the awkwardness hadn't disappeared after a few days. Tony still felt the shame that was not his fault but nonetheless seemed to be a fact of life he was going to be stuck with for a long time.

The phone rang as Kate started to talk again. Tony lifted the receiver, his back to her.

"Oh, hi, Chris. Yeah, things are going fine. . . ." He looked over at Kate, his smile tinged with irony.

"Thanks for the invite. I . . . I think I'll have

113

to take a rain check, though. Kate and I have already made plans. . . . Yeah, sure. Next time you get lucky. So long."

Kate picked the dishes up. The phone call had diffused Tony's flare-up. "Chris got a couple of tickets for a Bruins game from one of his clients."

Kate turned to him. "You're doing the same thing with Chris that you do with everybody else," she said hotly. "We don't have any plans. I have to pull teeth to get you to go to the movies, for God's sake. You're so afraid you'll run into somebody. . . ." She stormed off to the kitchen. Tony followed.

Her back to him, she said in a softer tone, "You're afraid to meet people, afraid to get close to anyone. Now you're even avoiding Chris."

He was behind her, his hands reaching round her chest. "I'm not afraid to get close to you," he said.

Kate wriggled out of his grasp, her eyes filled with tears. "You're willing to get close to me in bed."

"Kate . . ."

"Or as long as I keep our conversation on myself. But trying to get you to open up, to talk about your feelings, about . . . about so many things . . . is like struggling to open a can of sardines without the key."

"What do you want to know? Shall I tell you about life in prison? Now, that would be an eye-opener—the seamy happenings of the cons and

114

guards behind bars. How about the spot checks, the sadistic humor of a few of the guys, the body searches when something has been swiped? Or if that doesn't interest you, I could talk about work, about how it feels to have everybody looking at me in that funny way, bending over backwards to convince me that they trust me implicitly. Then there are the whispers . . . the new people at the place being told the sad saga of Tony Fielding. Be extra nice to the guy, he's had it rough. Rough? As if they could begin to know. As if anybody could."

Kate ran her tongue over dry lips. Her eyes were glistening with tears. "When does the nightmare end, Tony?" she asked softly.

He shook his head. "I wish I knew." He walked over and put his arms around her again, but they both felt the distance between them despite the embrace. His hands dropped to his sides. "I'm sorry, Katie. I start to think I'm getting things under control, and then . . ."

She swallowed, taking a deep breath. "It'll get better. We'll make it get better."

Neither of them was up for lovemaking that night, but they didn't want to be apart. In Tony's king-size bed Kate snuggled up against his warm body, slipping one hand under his neck, the other around his broad chest, and fell asleep.

It wasn't until several hours later that Tony was able to drift off. And when he did finally fall asleep, he slept so fitfully that he woke Kate up.

Her hand had gone numb beneath his neck, and

she carefully extracted it. Tony mumbled in his sleep. Kate pressed her hand to his chest in a soothing gesture. He was wet with perspiration. The mumbling grew louder, angry. He tugged at the covers as if they were suffocating him.

Kate shook him to wake him from his nightmare. He screamed out at her touch and sat up abruptly, fully awakening seconds later. He looked at her in sleepy confusion.

"It's all right," she said soothingly, easing him back onto the pillow. "Only a dream, a bad dream."

Tony mumbled something incoherent and immediately fell asleep once more. Kate tenderly drew his head to her shoulder. He reached over for her breast, cupping it contentedly in his sleep.

Kate sighed. When would the nightmare end?

After she finished reading over the statement, Kate looked up at Chris and then at Ron Delaney, the prosecuting attorney in the case of *The Commonwealth of Massachusetts* v. *Quinlan.*

"Everything seems right," she said, setting down the typewritten sheets. "When will she be brought to trial?"

"We have a tentative court date set for February third. The trial shouldn't run more than a week. I have you slated to give testimony the second day," Ron Delaney explained. "You, too, Chris."

Chris nodded. He hadn't seen Helen Quinlan behind the wheel the day she'd tried to run Kate down, but he could describe the car.

"I have no doubt of getting her on the embezzlement charge. I'm just hoping we can nail her on the attempted hit-and-run as well."

Chris saw that Kate had turned pale. He knew she had mixed feelings about that second charge. Chris had talked her into pressing charges, convincing her it was the right thing to do. Kate had agreed intellectually, but emotionally she felt disquieted about being the reason Helen Quinlan could do even more time.

"The judge may go easy on her," Chris said, pressing Kate's hand. "She could get a concurrent sentence, which would allow her to serve both prison terms at the same time . . . although, if you ask me, she deserves everything the judge can throw at her."

Kate nodded. "I know you both probably think I'm an idiot to feel sorry for the woman after what she did to me and to Tony. It's just that I don't think she ever meant to do it. That boyfriend of hers was behind the whole thing. Helen isn't the most beautiful woman," she said tactfully as the two men grinned. "Okay, she's an overweight, unattractive thirty-nine-year-old spinster. From the photo of her lover, Mitchell, that I saw in the paper, he was a guy who could have found a better catch. He certainly wasn't interested in Helen for her looks. All he wanted to do was manipulate her into getting him what he wanted."

"What some people will do for love." Ron sighed.

Chris looked over at Kate, who intentionally avoided his glance. She knew exactly what he was thinking. She'd made the mistake of crying on his shoulder about how rough things were going with Tony.

When they left Ron's office Chris took her arm. "It's your turn to buy me lunch."

"What?"

"That's so I don't get a firm 'No, thanks' by inviting you. You've been avoiding me lately, friend."

Kate started to protest as Chris led them to the elevator. "Tell me about it over a steak. You need some good red meat in you. Your eyes are starting to look watery, and your bones are beginning to sneak through your beautiful skin—both definite signs of protein deficiency," he teased gently as he pressed the down button of the elevator.

"You do know how to throw out the compliments, Counselor. Maybe you want to check my teeth and take my pulse."

He grabbed her wrist. "Hmmm. Just as I suspected." He turned her so that she was facing him. "You're skipping too many beats, even for a lady in love."

Kate shook her head. "You went into the wrong profession, Chris. You should have been a doctor."

They rode the crowded elevator in silence. He rushed her outside to beat out the competing cab grabbers, got a taxi right away, and gave the driver his home address.

"I thought you were taking me to lunch. I mean, I thought *I* was taking *you* to lunch," Kate amended.

"I remembered I have two steaks sitting in my fridge. If you cook, I'll count that as a buy."

Kate nodded, feeling a little funny about going back to Chris's apartment. She'd been there dozens of times, and he certainly wasn't taking her there now to show her the old etchings. She told herself to relax.

Chris Coleman lived in a converted town house on Pinckney Street, not far from Tony's Beacon Hill apartment. Tony knew that she and Chris were meeting with Ron Delaney that day and that Kate had taken the day off, not knowing how long the meeting would run. She had guessed that Chris would offer lunch and she had been all set to refuse him, just as Chris had surmised. But he had cleverly tricked her into cooperating.

During the short cab ride, Kate promised herself she was not going to end up crying on Chris's shoulder again. It wasn't fair to him or to Tony. If she and Tony were having problems, it wasn't right to wear out a good friend's shoulder because of it. Besides, Kate was trying to be sensitive to Chris's feelings for her, which she knew had grown stronger over the months they had worked together on Tony's case.

Chris opened the front door while Kate strug-

119

gled out of her leather boots. City grime would not go well with Chris's white carpet. He slipped his arm around her as she started to lose her balance.

"Thanks," she said, disconcerted by his touch.

Chris smiled easily. "Anytime."

When they stepped inside, he took her coat and offered her a drink. She shook her head and walked into the kitchen.

"Starving?" he asked, following her inside.

Kate stood at the open refrigerator door. "Not particularly."

He closed the door and took her hand, leading her back to the living room and over to the sofa. He shoved her gently onto a cushion and sat down beside her.

"Kate, you look lousy."

"More compliments?"

"You know what I'm talking about. You look beautiful . . . and lousy. Love is supposed to put a bloom in your cheeks, not make them turn pale."

"I'm not sleeping that well, that's all."

"How come?"

She started to give him a provocative answer but stopped herself. For one thing, she wasn't losing sleep lately because of long, heated nights of love-making with Tony. For another, it would be a cruel insinuation to throw in Chris's face, considering his feelings for her.

"Things seem to be getting worse instead of better," she said truthfully. "I thought time would be the great healer."

"I finally got Tony to go to a Bruins game with me the other night. He wasn't talking much, which is nothing new, but I could tell he isn't sleeping any better than you are."

"It's these awful nightmares he keeps having. They wake us both up," she said, confirming a suspicion Chris had had for months. They were spending most of their nights together. It didn't take a lawyer to figure out the obvious. Still, it hurt him to hear Kate refer to the intimacy she shared with Tony, even one racked with nightmares. He wanted to have that intimacy with her, and had found himself thinking about it more and more over the past few months.

Chris had always wanted Kate, but it had been a kind of game for a long time. He'd make his moves, laugh off the rebuffs, keep the friendship going all the while. Now he no longer felt like playing games. He'd been doing his best to accept the reality of Kate's feelings for Tony. If he'd hoped those feelings would fade once Tony was released from prison, he couldn't have been more off target. But he also could see that the relationship was in serious trouble. He cared about Kate enough to be sincerely upset for her, but he was honest enough with himself to know that he'd love to soothe her wounds if things didn't work out.

"How are things for Tony at work?" Chris asked, getting the conversation back on a less intimate subject. Kate had told him about the difficult adjustment Tony was having at Howell and Beck.

121

"As bad as before. He's trying, Chris, I know he is. We've had long talks about it. At first he was so defensive, but now he admits he's afraid to get close to people again. And the worse things get, the more he starts questioning our relationship, worrying about how I'm feeling."

She looked at Chris. "Sometimes it's so good. When he lets that damn guard of his down, he's like a different person."

Kate felt Chris's arm move around her shoulder, and she let herself lean against him. "We've decided to cool things a bit." She glanced up at Chris for a moment. "We both need to get some sleep. It's the practical thing to do, right?"

Chris squeezed her, his hand gently rubbing her arm.

Kate sighed. "I'd better cook up those steaks. My eyes are starting to water again."

CHAPTER SEVEN

"Hey, Tony . . . Tony Fielding."

Kate and Tony were walking out of a movie theater when they heard his name being shouted. Tony groaned as he recognized the man coming toward them.

"I didn't know you were . . . uh . . . Say, you look good, buddy. It's . . . it's been a while. I mean, I'm glad to see you're . . ." The man's hands rose and fell like a bird having trouble taking off as he floundered for words.

"How are you, Keith?"

"Good. Real good, Tony." He seemed relieved to get out one coherent sentence.

Tony turned toward Kate. "Kate Stuart . . . Keith Simmons."

Kate nodded. Keith extended his hand for a brief shake. The name sounded familiar, but she did not recognize the attractive dark-haired man.

"Nice to meet you, Miss Stuart." He looked back over at Tony. "My girl friend's holding our place in line for the next show. I ought to get back. It . . . was good to run into you."

As Keith Simmons turned to go, Tony said, "Give my regards to Jen."

Keith nodded, his smile awkward. Kate figured out another mystery. Keith Simmons . . . Jennifer Simmons.

She heard Tony inhale sharply as he started down the street several steps ahead of her.

"Are you taking this walk solo?" she quipped, trying for a light tone.

Tony slowed his pace. "Sorry. It's cold."

"You can say that again."

He ruffled her hair, then flung his arm around her shoulders. "I hate those encounters," he admitted. "The search for the right words, the heavy pauses, the eyes looking everyplace but at me."

"Especially when the encounter involves a relative of an ex-fiancée?"

"Brother."

Kate was quiet for a few minutes as they continued to walk down the street. "Let's stop for coffee," she suggested as they neared a small cafe.

Tony hesitated. He knew what was on Kate's mind—or, more accurately, who. Up until then, Tony had avoided any discussion of Jennifer Simmons. Jen was a part of his past, a past he'd just as soon forget. But his chance meeting with Keith reminded him that the past was still alive and flourishing in that town.

Kate was heading for the door of the restaurant, obviously making the decision for them. Tony walked in behind her. He quickly scanned the room for anyone he recognized, an instinct that had become all too natural for him. One encounter a night was enough—especially, as Kate had pointed out, when it was with the brother of one's ex-fiancée.

They slid into a booth. Kate kept her jacket on for warmth. She rubbed her hands together until Tony took them in his, providing his special brand of comfort.

They ordered coffee. Kate waited until the waitress brought over the two steaming mugs before she confronted Tony. "I want to talk about her."

Tony didn't respond.

"Jennifer Simmons," she said finally.

"I know who we're talking about."

"Who we're not talking about, you mean. Who we never talk about. Does it still hurt so much? Is that why I can always hear a pin drop when I so much as mention her name? Are you still—" She laughed wistfully. "Now I'm doing it . . . floundering for words."

He stroked her cheek with his cool fingers. "I keep trying to push my past aside, and it keeps right on following me around, catching me off guard." He looked down as Kate took his hand in hers. "Before everything went crashing down around me, I thought I had it made. Jen and I were supposed to be married a year ago August. Instead, on Sunday the seventh, I was sitting in jail, watching my world come apart at the seams.

"Jen comes from a very conservative middle-class family. They did not take too well to their future son-in-law turning out to be an accused embezzler. Suddenly I wasn't such a good catch," he said wryly.

"They couldn't believe you were guilty," Kate said.

"Well, that's a tricky issue. You see, if you're the kind of person who believes in truth, justice, and the American way, you believe a person is innocent only until proven guilty. The jury settled that one. Mr. and Mrs. Simmons had their doubts; I'll give them that much. But when it came down to the bottom line, that wasn't as important an issue as the fact that to the world at large I was guilty as charged. I was a con. There was no getting around that one."

"I presume Jen's a grown woman. She couldn't have been completely influenced by her parents. She had to draw her own conclusions."

Tony smiled. "Jen was as loyal as she could manage to be. She never believed I was guilty. For that I'll always be grateful. And she really tried to stick by me, despite the influence of her parents . . . and her friends. All through the trial she put up a brave front. But that was the problem: It was a front. She was playing the part of the loyal lover sticking by her man through thick and thin, for better or for worse. Only it was worse than she ever imagined."

Tony took a sip of his coffee. "It was terrible, for both of us. She was struggling to cope with it all, and I was struggling to ignore how hard she was struggling. When I reached the point where I couldn't ignore it any longer, I put an end to both our suffering."

"And Jen went along with it, just like that?"

"Katie," he said, reaching to touch her fine golden hair. "Everyone isn't as strong, as dedicated to a cause, as you."

"You're not a cause, Tony. You never were," she said, hurt by his remark, even though she knew he hadn't meant to hurt her. "I was attracted to you from that first day. Chris saw it; he didn't buy my denial for one minute. But he really didn't understand what the attraction was all about, any more than you seem to." She flushed slightly but kept her eyes on him. "Remember when you warned me about the effect I was having on your body that first time? Well, the effect you were having on mine was remarkably similar. I didn't have the excuse of being locked away for a year, which made it all the more startling for me. You are a very sexy man, Tony Fielding."

"So all this time it's been my body and not my innocence that's kept you going." He grinned at her.

"Your body . . . and your heart," she said softly, pressing her lips to his cheek. "I didn't fall in love with a cause. I fell in love with a man."

"A man with a past that keeps following him around," he murmured.

"And a present that I don't think he gives enough weight to," Kate said pointedly.

"You haven't won yourself a prize, Kate. I know I've said it before, but I still think you're getting the short end of the stick."

"I'm the last person to say you're perfect, Mr. Fielding," she replied. "You have a hot temper, you can get rather maudlin at times, and your head is occasionally thick. Not to mention your being stubborn, reclusive—"

"Whoa! The stick is getting shorter by the second."

Kate cupped his chin. "I've seen you at your worst . . . and at your best. Your best is pretty damn terrific. You see, I really do believe in 'for better or for worse.' "

"I know you do, Katie. That's what I keep banking on." He ran his index finger over her lips, then kissed her tenderly.

Kate felt as if a huge weight had been lifted, as if spring were in the air right there in the middle of November. If someone came along at that moment and told her that her wonderful sense of well-being would be shattered in less than forty-eight hours, she would have dismissed him as crazy.

On Monday morning Kate found a memo on her desk asking her to meet with Jud Howell at ten o'clock. She jotted the time down on her calendar and rescheduled her nine-thirty meeting with her staff. Mr. Howell probably wanted to check on how she was doing with the tedious process of straightening out the accounts Helen Quinlan had so cleverly manipulated. It was slow going, but Kate, having assumed sole responsibility for the project, had just finished up. She'd first had to wait for the FBI to conclude their audit; otherwise she might have got done weeks sooner.

Jud Howell's office was on the twenty-eighth floor, the windows of his oatmeal-carpeted room offering a fine view of the Boston skyline. Kate hadn't been up there since that awful day when Helen had roared toward her in her Triumph.

"Good morning, Miss Stuart. Please sit down." Mr. Howell stood formally, pointing to a comfortable taupe leather armchair. "How are the rectifications coming along?"

"They're complete, I'm happy to say."

"Quite a task," Jud Howell agreed, sweeping his hand across his gray hair. "We're very grateful, Miss Stuart, for everything you've done, but then, I've told you that several times over the past six weeks. I hate to think what might have happened —who might have suffered this time—if you hadn't been so alert and so persistent."

"There's certainly been enough suffering as it is," Kate said.

"Yes . . . Fielding. I don't think I'll ever get over having helped send an innocent man to prison for all those months."

Kate felt like saying Tony wouldn't ever get over

129

it, either, but she realized Jud Howell was sincerely upset. She kept her mouth shut.

"I've had several meetings with the board about you, Miss Stuart. We feel a promotion is in order. The general policy, as you know, is to consider promotions only after an employee has been with us for one year, but you certainly do not fit any general policy. So, on behalf of the board, I'd like to offer you an executive-officer position. It means not only an ample salary increase but a voice at executive meetings, an office on this floor, and a chance to help us establish more effective processing controls. We can't afford to lose credibility in this business, as I'm sure you understand. We have great faith in your ability to work with us to see that that won't happen."

"I'm not usually speechless, Mr. Howell . . . but for once in my life I don't know what to say."

"Say 'Yes, of course.'"

Kate gave him a wide grin. "Yes . . . of course."

"Good. Then let me welcome you to this floor, Kate." He stood up, walked around the desk, and shook her hand.

"Thank you . . . Jud."

"Yes, I think things are going to work out just fine. I'll have my secretary, Marion, show you your new quarters. If there's anything you need or want, tell Marion and she'll make sure that you get it."

Marion appeared at the doorway as Jud and Kate shook hands once more.

"Oh, I'm planning a little welcome party for you. It's standard procedure." He smiled. "Marion will let you know the date tomorrow."

The ever-efficient Marion nodded and led Kate down the hall to her new suite.

"Why won't you come with me?"

"Kate, please, for once let go of something. It's not jealousy . . . it's not embarrassment . . . it's not reclusiveness."

"Then what is it?"

Tony shrugged. "Did you ever think it might be utterly boring for me or that I've made other plans?"

"Made other plans? You didn't mention anything when I told you about the party this afternoon."

Tony studied her, grim-faced. Why had he set things up like this? Did he unconsciously mean to hurt her? Or himself? He didn't want to tell her this way, not with them both careening toward another blowup. But he had walked right into it.

"Katie . . ."

She didn't like the sound of his voice or the rigid set of his jaw. She waited, trying not to roll her hands into fists.

"I had a call at the office after we talked about your party." He was having trouble meeting her steady gaze. "From Jen . . . Jennifer Simmons."

131

Tony had the urge to clear his throat, but he didn't want to draw more attention to his nervousness. "Keith told her we'd bumped into each other outside that movie theater." He wished Kate wouldn't sit there looking like she was waiting for a verdict to be handed down. He came over to her, resting his hands on her shoulders. "Jen asked me to meet her for a drink. I agreed."

"For Saturday night," Kate muttered.

"I told you this afternoon I didn't want to go to the party, so when Jen suggested Saturday, I said okay."

Kate turned away, but Tony gripped her more firmly, refusing to let her go. "You're always the one telling me not to turn away from my past, Kate. Well, Jen is a part of that past—a part I left hanging."

"Oh," Kate snapped, "I thought that was one you'd resolved."

He narrowed his eyes. "You can't resolve anything in a prison waiting room."

"No. No, I guess you can't," she said sullenly.

"Kate, the only purpose of this get-together is to close the books on a better note."

"Does she know you were acquitted?"

"I told her, naturally."

"Naturally," she echoed sarcastically.

"Hey, you're the reasonable one, remember? Levelheaded, rational . . ."

"What would you like me to do? Step aside and tell you I think it's great that you and the woman

132

you wanted to marry last year are about to have a friendly little reunion. Damn it, Tony, what makes you think I have no jealous bones in my body? Well, let me tell you, I've got plenty. I don't like Jen moving in on my territory. She walked out when you were down, if you've forgotten. But now . . . now you've been exonerated. You're a free man. So I guess you're free to do what you damn well please. Only don't you dare expect me to be reasonable about it."

She tried to struggle out of his grasp, but he tightened his hold. "Wait one second, Miss Stuart. It seems to me you expect me to be reasonable about your friendly get-togethers with Chris Coleman," he said, glaring at her. "I think one reasonable turn deserves another, don't you?"

"Chris is a friend. He was a friend long before I ever met you."

"So was Jen," he countered.

"I was never intimately involved with Chris."

"That could change. There's always the possibility, especially inasmuch as the man is crazy about you."

"I'm crazy about you," Kate said forlornly.

"Katie, I love you too. But I have to see Jen. We'd be bound to bump into each other one of these days. I think both of us want to avoid the terrible awkwardness of that kind of chance meeting."

Kate nodded, letting Tony take her in his arms, her anger drifting into a sad disquiet. Why was it every time she thought things were starting to look up, a strong wind came along and pushed her down to peg one again?

Kate told herself it wasn't spite at all that had made her ask Chris to the welcome reception for her that Saturday night. The invitation had resulted in another squabble with Tony, but he didn't have much of a case, considering his own plans for the evening. Kate had told Tony she did not want to show up alone at the party, and Chris was the only other man she knew well enough to ask.

Chris was pleased about the invitation. He hadn't seen Kate very much over the past couple of weeks. They'd both been busy, and Kate had become increasingly uneasy about getting together for friendly lunches. Chris missed her. When she asked him to the party, explaining only that Tony had other plans, he responded with an immediate, enthusiastic yes.

"You look too beautiful for that group of stuffed shirts," Chris whispered as he led her into the elegant private dining room at the Copley Plaza Hotel. "What do you say we make an early exit and I show you off at some swank night spot?"

"This party's for me, pal. I don't think they'd appreciate their guest of honor sneaking off early."

Jud Howell walked over to greet them, putting an arm around Kate's shoulder after pumping Chris's hand. "Lovely dress, Kate. We've never

134

had such a pretty executive officer join our folds. Don't tell Laura Gladstone I said that, though." Laura Gladstone was executive personnel officer and the only other female in a top-level position at Howell and Beck. Laura was in her fifties, wafer-thin and a fire-breathing dynamo. In the looks department she was no competition for Kate.

Kate was the youngest member of the executive group, as well as only the second woman to be instated in the upper echelons. She could tell by the greetings which members of the fold welcomed her openly and which held some reservations. On one issue everyone was unanimous: They all agreed that Kate had almost single-handedly averted a terrible disaster. Some of the execs would have preferred it if she had received a whopping bonus, leaving it at that. Kate was glad there were enough people at the party who viewed her as an asset and not merely an adornment for the twenty-eighth floor.

Several times during the formal, rather tedious sit-down dinner, she caught Chris looking pain-fully weary as he engaged in conversation with one of the more long-winded vice-presidents. He re-vived whenever Kate gave him a sympathetic smile. Chris was a good sport to come along with her. Tony had been right about one thing: He would have been horribly bored. She forced thoughts of Tony from her mind. Right now he was sitting next to Jennifer Simmons in some cozy bar. . . . She motioned to the waiter for another martini.

People started drifting out after dinner. By ten o'clock all but a few of the more hearty drinking crowd had left. Chris convinced Kate that no one remaining among the glassy-eyed group would miss her at that point. They said their good-byes and exchanged more vigorous handshakes. One of the VPs planted a rather intemperate kiss smack on Kate's lips.

"You're going to have to watch that Nelson guy." Chris grinned. "I think he's mighty hot on you."

"He's mighty drunk," Kate giggled. "By Monday morning he won't remember a thing about it. Come to think of it, I probably won't, either."

Chris slipped his arm through hers. "There's a nice band playing our song in the Carousel Lounge of this place. Want to take a spin around the dance floor with me?"

"What's our song?" Kate quipped.

Chris smiled at her. "I could think of a few, but I'll take whatever one they're playing when we walk in."

They were playing an old familiar love song. Chris pulled Kate into his arms. "Dance with me anyway."

He held her close, working hard at keeping himself in check—which wasn't easy, considering how good Kate's slender body felt pressed against his. As the song neared its end he considered throwing caution to the winds and making one grand pitch for her.

As they settled down at the bar Kate looked around the room and then turned to Chris. "Tony's meeting his ex-fiancée tonight at some bar. I suddenly had this sick feeling it might be this one. I don't think I'm up to coping with sweet Jen." She gave Chris a mournful smile.

Chris forgot about the pitch he was working on, realizing the timing couldn't be worse.

"I thought Jennifer Simmons was out of the picture."

"So did I. We ran into her brother the other night, and the next day she called Tony and asked to get together with him."

"You sound pretty understanding."

"Don't use that word or you might see stars. I am definitely, absolutely, unequivocally, *not* understanding about any of it. However, my permission wasn't being requested. Tony Fielding is a free man. That's what I told him. I said, 'Tony. You are a free man.' That's right, isn't it, Counselor?"

Chris eyed her quizzically. "How many of those martinis did you drink downstairs?"

Kate began counting on her fingers. She stopped at the pinky. "Now I'm not sure about the pinky. I think I only drank half of that one." She put her hand to her mouth. "I'm not slurring, am I? I absolutely hate slurring drunks."

Chris smiled. "Come on, I'm taking you home."

137

"No, wait. They're playing our song. One more dance. I'm just getting warmed up."

"I see. That's what I'm afraid of. These romantic tunes are giving me ideas. If we keep dancing, I can't say I won't try some of them out."

She cocked her head, her lips curved into a broad smile. "I think I get what you mean."

"Good. Then let's go home."

"Did Tony ever tell you about the time he threw up in his third-grade class? He was very embarrassed. I think I'd like to try to make it to the powder room. That way neither of us will be too humiliated."

"Good idea," he said, grabbing her arm and racing out of the bar, depositing her at the door to the ladies' room.

Ten minutes later a paler but more steady Kate stepped out the door. "I'm still embarrassed," she said softly, meeting Chris's concerned gaze. "But I feel better." She managed a weak smile.

"Neither of us will remember it in the morning," Chris said, squeezing her hand warmly.

"You're a real pal, Chris." Kate sighed, resting her head on his shoulder for a moment before he half carried her to the elevator.

Tony was already sitting at a small table at the cocktail lounge a half hour before he was supposed to meet Jen. He wanted some time to calm his nerves and think about why he had agreed to meet with her, what he hoped to accomplish. There was an incessant drone from the singles gathered around the bar. A year ago this place had been almost deserted on a Saturday night. That's why Tony had suggested it. But now it had become one of the new "in" spots. Not the best setting for this particular reunion.

He spotted Jen immediately as she made her way through the crowd. Attentive male eyes followed her gliding progress across the room. Jen always drew stares. She had the kind of beauty that exuded breeding, the finest finishing schools, and lots of money. None of that was true, but she carried the image off wonderfully. Tonight Jen looked as regal as ever, her thick, dark mane of hair swept back in a finely coiled figure-eight–shaped knot. She was five feet nine inches tall, so she towered over most of the women at the lounge. But Jen wasn't the type to minimize her height. She was as straight as an arrow, reed-thin, with the bearing of a princess. She had shoulders that were almost never hunched. But Tony had seen them that way—during the ordeal of his trial and those few brief meetings in the prison.

She stopped a few feet from him as he pushed his chair back and stood up. They stared at each other, each unsure about how to begin. Tony took the initiative. He walked over, gave her a peck on the cheek, and, taking her elbow, steered her to a chair.

"It's nice to see you, Jen. You look as beautiful as ever."

"Thanks, Tony. You look good yourself, especially considering where you've been hanging out this past year."

At least there was going to be no awkward hemming and hawing. That was a relief.

Jen took his hand. "You have no idea how happy I was to hear you were finally acquitted. Why couldn't they have figured that out last year before they put you through hell?"

Tony decided not to get into how Kate had come along and rescued him from hell. That wasn't the purpose of this meeting.

"I have to count my lucky stars it happened at all."

"Over these past months I've thought about you so much, Tony. There's this sense of guilt . . . of having failed you . . . that's never stopped haunting me. I knew I had to see you again, to try to explain. . . ."

"I don't need explanations, Jen. Anyway, that's not really where it's at. You didn't agree to marry a convicted felon."

"I knew you were innocent. I never stopped believing in you."

"You might have known, but there would always be those who didn't have your firm convictions. You had to be thinking about that. About how you would deal with those people—say, at

140

cocktail parties or office get-togethers . . . or weddings."

"You sound bitter."

Tony had to laugh. "I'm not bitter at you, Jen. You did what was best."

"Best for me, you mean."

"That's what I thought then. But now it's finally clear to me that it was best for both of us. It would have been a festering wound between us that would never have healed."

He looked over at her, a lot of things coming into focus. "Prison was no picnic, but in some ways being out is rougher. I've been trying these last couple of months to recapture a past that existed before all of this insanity happened. But you know something, Jen? You can't turn back the clock. Nor can you keep it from moving forward. It's finally hit me that's what I've been trying to do: fit back into a groove that's shifted with time. I don't fit anymore. I've got to find someplace where I do."

"You've changed, Tony," Jen said wistfully. "For the better, I think," she added with a warm smile. "You've turned introspective, more sensitive. But I don't feel like we know each other anymore. I guess that makes me feel sad. I don't know . . . maybe I came here tonight to see if I could turn back the clock too. But all that's happened is it's fifteen minutes later than when I first walked in the door."

141

"So, what do you say we have a drink and toast both our futures."

"That sounds like a good idea," she agreed.

"Gin gimlet?"

She nodded. "A few things never change."

CHAPTER EIGHT

It was one of Tony's more awkward encounters, but it had nothing to do with his recent personal history. After his brief date with Jen, he'd walked over to Kate's place, let himself into her apartment with the key she had given him, and waited for her to get home from her business dinner. As he sat in her living room at eleven-fifteen that Saturday night, he watched the front door swing open, Kate ensconced in the arms of Chris Coleman. Both men stood facing each other, speechless. Kate, roused by the light in the apartment, lifted her head up from Chris's shoulder, smiled sweetly at both men, and slumped down again.

"She had a little too much to drink." Chris looked around for a place to set her. He finally opted for the couch, having to disentangle Kate's hands from around his neck. He gave Tony a crooked smile. "Next time, make sure she stops at her index finger."

"What?"

"Never mind. Just keep her away from martinis altogether."

Tony nodded, at a loss for words. He couldn't decide if he owed Chris an explanation for being there or if Chris owed him one. He would also have liked some kind of explanation from Kate, but she was definitely not up for explaining anything.

"Well, I guess I'll be off, then," Chris said, heading for the door. "You made the right decision about not going to that dinner. Duller than Saturday-night TV. Big drinkers, those execs. Half of them were under the table when we left." He omitted the two dances around the floor. "They kept plying Kate with booze, but she was no match for them. She probably won't be feeling too great tomorrow morning."

"Yeah, well, I'll get her to bed. Um, thanks, Chris," he said, still not sure he should be thanking him. Chris had looked real happy having Kate snug in his arms—until he saw Tony staring at him. Had he been planning to tuck her in himself?

Tony felt strong proprietary rights to Kate. He may have given lip service to Kate being better off with a guy like Chris, who was stable and settled, with no ghosts to fight. But when he saw Kate in Chris's arms, he knew he didn't mean it. Tony loved her. As difficult as things were for them, tonight he had begun to see the light at the end of the tunnel. There were some big changes necessary, but he felt more optimistic now about his future with Kate than he had before.

He walked Chris to the door, both of them

mumbling awkward good-byes. Tony turned back and gazed at Kate, sprawled out on the living-room couch.

She raised one hand, her index finger beckoning, eyes still closed.

"I thought you'd passed out," Tony said, walking over to her.

She opened one eye. "I can, too, make it past my index finger. Two martinis are nothing," she said, her words just a bit slurred. "Now, maybe that third one was going too far." She raised her next finger, then giggled, making a fist. "Come over here. What's taking you so long?"

He knelt down beside her on the couch. She tilted her head toward him, opening both eyes. She was tipsy, but not as far gone as Tony had thought. "How's sweet Jen?"

"Sweet."

"I still don't like her."

"To tell you the truth," he whispered, "I'm not particularly crazy about her myself."

"You're not?"

He shook his head, then took her in his arms. "I'm crazy about you."

She placed her hands on his shoulders. "You don't have any other ex-fiancées hidden in your closet, do you?"

"There's no one else."

"Prove it." She gave him her most lascivious grin.

"Katie . . ."

145

"I'm not as drunk as you think," she whispered, her hands traveling down his chest to the waist-band of his trousers.

"You aren't going to remember a thing in the morning," he said, then gasped as her hands slipped lower.

"If I don't," she said, tracing the outline of his lips with the tip of her tongue before continuing, "you can refresh my memory. Besides, this way I can be as wanton as I want and I can pretend it's that third martini. . . ." She raised her finger again.

Tony laughed. Kate began to kiss his neck voraciously, struggling all the while to undress him as he knelt beside her.

"Help me a little, will you?" She breathed hotly into his ear. "I'm not at my most coordinated just now."

"Allow me," he murmured into her wind-tossed hair, slipping his shirt off and then standing for a moment to get out of the rest of his clothes.

Kate looked up, her eyes traveling slowly over his body. Then her hands reached out for him, stroking him with possessive tenderness. Tony bent down, gathered her in his arms, and carried her into the bedroom.

He helped her out of her clothes. He placed her on the bed, then slipped the warm down quilt over both of them.

She snuggled next to him and immediately proceeded to fall asleep. Tony grinned. Some wanton hussy!

Light was streaming into the room. Tony turned onto his stomach and tried to pull the covers over his head, but they wouldn't budge. He tried again.

"Give up."

Tony opened his eyes to see Kate, dressed in a provocatively sheer nightgown, holding one edge of the quilt. On the side table was a tray laid out with orange juice, coffee, and hot rolls.

He closed his eyes again, but Kate's hand languorously trailed along the length of his body.

"You're supposed to have a whopping hangover."

"I do." She grinned as he turned over to look up at her. "I was hoping you'd have a cure."

"You conked out on my cure last night," Tony murmured, his hand softly stroking her breast over the thin lacy gown.

"I did? And here I was, thinking we had ourselves a really terrific time."

"Do you know that you snore when you're in a drunken stupor?" he said teasingly, his hands moving down to her thighs.

"You're cruel when you've been denied, Mr. Fielding," she teased back.

"It's a very sexy snore." He pulled her down on top of him. "Warm me up. You owe me."

"I do, do I?"

"Mmm-hmm."

"There's hot coffee. . . ."

"Not what I need." His lips proceeded to nibble at her shoulders, and then their lips found each other's, the teasing playfulness vanishing as passion shot through them. Tony rolled her over on her back, still kissing her, moving with her. He began to fumble with the soft silk gown entangled around her body.

Lifting his head, he looked down at her. "How much did this nightgown cost you?"

"What? I don't—Forty dollars, I think."

"Good. Put it on my bill. I owe you forty bucks," he said; then, with a force that both startled and excited Kate, he ripped the gown down the center.

"Wanton," she whispered in his ear. "Very wanton."

He tossed the ripped gown onto the floor, then cupped her breasts in his broad hands, delighting in the hardening pressure of her nipples against his palms.

He slid down between her thighs, his hands stroking, exploring, taunting, so that she began to make faint, breathy whimpering sounds. His lips skimmed across her firm stomach. He could feel her quiver. Her back arched and she moaned louder.

Kate shuddered, ecstatic, as she felt his tongue glide over her trembling flesh. He was gentle but insistent as she squirmed beneath him, determined to make her yield fully to the fierce mounting pleasure she was feeling. He slipped his hands around her buttocks, lifting her to him. Her fingers dug into his shoulders, her cries stronger, more urgent, pleading now, oblivious to anything but the burning passion about to explode inside of her. Quick, shallow breaths . . . and then an abandoned cry of exquisite release.

He rested his head against her chest, listening to her rapid heartbeat. She locked him in her embrace, her legs wrapped tightly around his thighs, not wanting to risk his moving off of her. He slipped a still-hard nipple between his lips, delighting in Kate's murmur of pleasure as he gently sucked. She ran her long fingers through his hair, then down to his shoulders, her nails scratching lightly against his muscular back. He slid up higher, reaching her lips, kissing her lightly at first, then more deeply as her hands began to set his body on fire, throbbing, wanting. . . .

"Katie . . . I love you." His tongue circled hers as their lips met again.

Their bodies joined, and Kate thrilled to the feel of the man she loved, warm inside of her, a part of her, vital, strong, carrying her again to that intense point of sheer ecstasy.

Later, still entwined in each other's arms, Tony murmured, "How's your head?"

"What head?" Kate giggled like a young child. "I lost it over an hour ago. No, I think I lost it two months back." She hugged him tighter. "Oh, Tony, I feel like this is finally the peace after the storm." She squinted up at him, her fingers gently touching his lips. "Who'd ever guess I could feel so terrific after all those martinis I managed to down at that party?" She paused for a moment, her smile fading. "You had me worried for a while there last night. I was pretty jealous."

"No kidding," he teased.

"And I'm not ashamed of it," she said with a glint in her eye. "I don't want to lose you."

She spotted the barest glimmer of a frown on his face. Then he gave her an affectionate slap on her butt. "Come on, get up. I'll make you a real breakfast." He bent over to retrieve her nightgown and then remembered what he'd done to it. He slipped out of bed, stepped into his slacks, and walked over to the closet for her robe. He tossed it onto the bed, but Kate made no move to put it on or get out of bed. Instead she sat there, arms crossed, her eyes fixed on him.

"What aren't you talking about?"

"Katie." He sighed. "I thought we said no more storms."

"I thought so too." Her eyes narrowed. "But then, every time I think we've made it over the finish line, I get this uneasy sense somebody's putting up another ribbon."

"Let's have something to eat and we'll talk. You do amaze me, Katie. Nothing ever does get by you. What was it—the change in my breathing pattern, the look in my eye, the tone of my voice?"

"You were supposed to say 'You won't lose me,

Katie.' That's the way my script read. Obviously you're working from a different one."

He came back and sat down on the bed. "You won't lose me, Katie. It's just that first I have to find myself."

"No," she moaned, "not that again." She grabbed her robe, put it on, and strode out of the room.

"Kate? Can we please talk like two civilized people, without the storm?"

"I thought we were going to have breakfast." She was already heading through the living room to the kitchen.

"I'll do it," he said as she slammed the butter dish onto the counter. "If you treat the eggs that way, we'll have ourselves quite a mess."

"We do already," she snarled, but let him take over the cooking.

He fried a couple of eggs, reheated the coffee, and buttered two rolls, setting everything on the kitchen table. Kate adjusted the blinds, allowing only a modicum of morning sunlight into the room. She didn't feel that the day called for much brightness, considering the shadows cast over her ebullient mood.

They ate in silence. Kate was not really hungry but didn't know what else to do. Tony kept glancing over at her, hoping the food would soften the scowl that had furrowed her forehead. It didn't.

"Katie . . ." he began as soon as they had nothing left on their plates.

151

She regarded him coolly. "Save the affectionate approach. You're cutting out, aren't you?"

He looked shocked.

"It didn't take any great brilliance to deduce that one," she told him. "You've talked about finding yourself before, remember? How you can't do it here, surrounded by a lot of people who keep reminding you of where you spent the past year."

"That is what's happening. Every day. You can see yourself that it's not getting easier. I . . . I feel trapped here, Kate."

So it was *Kate* now. She sighed. "New York, right?"

"If I told you I want you to come with me . . ."

"You know the answer." Her tone was sad, resigned. She wasn't going to talk him out of it this time. All her efforts to date had won only a temporary reprieve.

"I have to do this, Kate. I don't fit in at Howell and Beck anymore. It's not even the people; it's the work itself. Before the whole business with the embezzlement came up, I was your typical up-and-comer. I slaved away forty to fifty hours a week, knocking myself out to increase my figures, lure new customers. I went to sleep with the Dow-Jones averages swimming in my head. I made a good living, had the respect of my peers, the admiration of my fiancée . . . but I was too busy even to stop to ask myself if I was happy. Those fourteen months locked away—I thought about them a

152

lot. I thought of all the things I missed, the things I never tried, the dreams I used to dream way back when I was a kid."

"Why can't we make those dreams come true together?" Kate asked softly. She understood Tony's dilemma and wanted to be part of the solution.

He walked over to her and drew her up from her chair. "Katie, you can help me more than I think you realize to make those dreams come true. I want you, but I have to offer you something whole, something I value. I need to get rid of these nightmares, the moodiness that seems to hit me when I least expect it. I'm fighting against tidal waves here. Pete is offering me the opportunity to be my own man. I won't have to explain anything to anyone. That's the freedom I crave. It's a truly fresh start."

"Where do I fit into this fresh start?"

"Other people manage to keep a relationship going over a few hundred miles. We can spend our weekends together, holidays . . ."

"I've already tried that once."

The doorbell rang. Tony dropped his arms from Kate's shoulders and she went to answer it.

"Hi. I met your next-door neighbor in the lobby and he let me in." Chris looked from Kate to Tony, who was standing in the kitchen doorway. "I guess I should have buzzed."

"No. Don't be silly. Come on in."

"I was just bringing your purse back. I didn't

remember till I was taking my jacket off at home that you'd asked me to tuck it into my pocket."

Kate took the tiny gold mesh purse with a nod. Chris was still standing at the door. "Well, I'm off, then."

"No, come have a cup of coffee. Or maybe a toast is more in order," she said stonily. "A bon-voyage toast."

"Oh?" Chris looked back to Tony again.

Tony came into the living room. "I've been trying to explain to Kate that I . . ." He threw up his hands. "What's the use?"

"Tony's quitting Howell and Beck. He's going to find himself in New York." She turned from Chris, giving Tony an icy stare as she strode into her bedroom.

Another awkward encounter. Tony sat slumped in a chair. Chris was still poised at the door. He probably should turn and leave. This wasn't his fight. Didn't he say he no longer wanted to be monkey in the middle?

"Have some coffee," Tony said with a weak smile. "Pour one for me too."

So much for bowing out of the triangle. Chris walked into the kitchen, poured two cups of black coffee, and carried them back into the living room.

"Thanks," Tony said, taking the mug from Chris's outstretched hand. "Sit down. You make me nervous. I'm tense enough."

"As they say, 'You could cut it with a knife.'"

Tony grimaced.

"Sorry. Crises bring out the triteness in me."

"I don't hold up too well under them myself," Tony admitted. "What is it about Kate and me? Half the time we're floating on cloud nine—see, buddy, I can be as trite as the next guy—and the next minute we're taking up arms to do battle." He pressed his palms against his temples. "The problem is, I'm not just another guy. Fourteen months ago I was. Fourteen months ago I was an ordinary Joe—no nightmares, no sordid past, no prison record written in indelible ink on my forehead."

"Fourteen months ago, old pal, you were about to be married to another woman, and I was figuring out a terrific new approach to try on Kate Stuart. So don't give me this crap about the past. You want to go find yourself in New York, you have my blessing. I'd be a fool to try to convince you it could be dangerous to leave a lady like Kate behind. I plan to be the danger. Just to keep everything clear between us . . . friend."

"Kate's a big girl. She has the right to make her own choices."

"Choice about what?" Kate asked.

Startled, both men looked up to see Kate walk back into the room. She was dressed in jeans and a plaid flannel shirt. She stuck one foot on the arm of Tony's chair to tie the lace of her sneaker. When she finished, she put up the other foot. "I certainly know how to make an entry," she remarked sarcastically.

Chris stood up, placing his untouched coffee

mug on the table. "Given my choices, I think I'll bid you both a fond farewell. Sunday is my day off."

"Mine too," Kate said. She walked over to Chris, gave him an affectionate hug, and opened the door for him. After he walked out, she closed the door and turned to Tony. "I'm in the mood for a long walk. Care to join me?"

Tony came up to her, eyeing her with caution. "Somehow I don't trust this calm after the storm."

"There's nothing not to trust," Kate said dispassionately. "You've made your decision; I'm trying to make the best of it. I considered my choices as I got dressed. I could rant and rave again—a skill I must admit I'm becoming quite proficient at—or burst into tears and try to drown you in them, or accept the inevitable. You're the one who is always telling me I'm a rational person. So I'm being rational." She gave him a huffy stare, her foot tapping rhythmically on the rug.

Tony wanted to take her in his arms and hug her. She was trying so hard. Instead he said, "Can you wait until I put on my shirt?"

They walked along the quiet paths of the Arnold Arboretum. In the spring this was a lush wonderland of ornamental trees and shrubs. Now most of the limbs were bare as late autumn gave way to winter. There was a bleakness to the place that both Kate and Tony felt as well as observed.

He had his arm around her. For the past half

hour he'd talked about his brother Pete's real estate business and the kind of opportunities it offered him. Kate listened quietly, hands dug into the pockets of her jacket. It was chilly but windless, making the long walk tolerable.

"Pete's a terrific guy. You'll meet him when you come down. His wife, Sheila, can be a little overbearing at times, but she means well. She just likes to fuss over people. They've got themselves a nice place in Westchester County, maybe thirty minutes from midtown Manhattan. Pete's mostly been operating out of the city, but he's spreading into Westchester and even Connecticut. That's where I fit in: He wants me to take over some of the newer markets. Meanwhile, I'll have to take a real estate course so I can get my license. . . . Katie, are you listening?"

She stopped walking and looked over at Tony. "You sound happy." She pursed her lips. "I feel totally rotten . . . and yet, it feels good to hear you talk enthusiastically. It feels good to see you brimming with optimism, looking excited, eager. . . ." Tears burned at the corners of her eyes. "I guess love has its few selfless moments." She smiled weakly. "Don't expect them to last too long."

Tony took her in his arms and kissed her again and again until, breathless, she pulled away. "This could be the beginning of the end," she said, the note of despair back in her voice.

"I don't see it that way."

"When are you going?"

"I'll have to give the company a couple of weeks' notice. I know Pete's ready for me to start whenever I can get there." He saw her frown, her quick accusatory glance.

"I've had a few long talks on the phone with Pete. Older brother to younger brother and all that. He knows the kind of pressure, the strain, I've felt being back here."

"Does he think moving away is the answer?" Kate asked, not bothering to mask the edge in her voice, those few selfless moments having already evaporated.

"He thinks I have to make my own decisions. He's willing to back me in whatever I do."

Kate started walking again, feeling like an intangible conspiracy was developing around her. She quickened her pace.

Tony forced her to stop, his hand grasping her wrist. "Listen to me: I love you. I'm going to love you in New York just as much as I do in Boston. We don't have to be together every day to validate our feelings, do we?" His voice was angry, tinged with frustration.

"It isn't validation I need. Oh, Tony, don't you see? I'm another piece of your past. You were a convict when I fell in love with you. We had our courtship in a prison waiting room, for God's sake. I'm a reminder. . . . I'm a thread leading back to memories you're running clear to New York to get away from. You want a new life, a new identity.

158

Damn it, I'd always be there remembering the . . . the real you, the man filled with suffering, pain, nightmares . . . the man whose depth and sensitivity and tenderness have spoiled me rotten."

He held her against him. "Come with me, Kate. There are good jobs in New York. You are the only part of that past I want to hold on to—the only part I need."

Kate shook her head, her eyes moist. "I can't, Tony. There's lots of reasons, but the most important one is that I think what you're doing is a mistake. I don't believe in new identities or running away from the past. I believe in confronting ghosts, scaring the bloody hell out of them, letting them know who's boss. Your mother was right, all those years back, when she said you had nothing to be ashamed of. You don't have to cringe whenever you meet someone in the street who doesn't know what to say. Damn it, you haven't done anything. You haven't committed any crime."

Tony glared at her, his face red with rage. "You go spend a year of your life in jail as an accused felon and then come talk to me about not feeling shame. You tell me you can ignore the looks, the whispers behind your back. You know what my biggest mistake was: not leaving for New York when I meant to. . . ." He stopped, catching his breath, seeing the pain etched in her face. "Katie, I didn't mean—"

"Forget it, Tony."

"No. I'm not going to let us destroy what we

have—what we're going to have. I only meant that if I'd gone to New York a few months ago, I might have worked out some of the bitterness, the confusion, the sense of feeling so disconnected. Maybe we wouldn't have locked horns so much then."

"Not as often anyway," Kate said wryly.

"Can't you accept the fact that the more self-confidence I feel, the better it will be for the two of us?"

She didn't want to argue anymore. Sure, there was that possibility. There was also the possibility that Tony would create a new life for himself . . . and discover there wasn't any room in it for her.

She struggled to hide her doubts and fears. As he bent down to capture her lips she told herself it was a kiss filled with a promise. A promise she prayed Tony meant to keep.

CHAPTER NINE

Kate showed her pass to the guard sitting at the desk in the otherwise desolate lobby. It was Saturday morning, and the twenty-eighth floor of the Seaton Building was the last place Kate wanted to be on this bleak, snowy December day. As he marked her name and the time down in the ledger, the guard yawned, mirroring Kate's feelings perfectly.

There was only one elevator working during off-hours. Kate pressed the button. The door opened immediately. She leaned against a wall, letting her own yawn escape. *That's what you get for climbing up the corporate ladder,* she thought, and sighed. Sixty hours of work a week instead of forty. She'd asked for it, taking on the extra hours with a vengeance at first.

Anything to counteract the loneliness. Deep down she had known it would be this way. She bought Tony's promises only because she so desperately wanted to believe everything would work out the way he had said. Every weekend . . . certainly every other. . . .

First he'd said he had to settle in. Pete wanted to show him the ropes. "Look, honey, Pete works Monday through Friday, and often on weekends. I have to be available when it's good for him." Good-bye to the first few weekends. Then there was the real estate course. That was Saturdays. And then he had to study . . . and then he realized weekends were a good time to meet clients. . . .

He missed her. He told her often enough—on the phone. In the five weeks he'd been gone, they'd been together only once. And on that one precious weekend, he'd brought work with him. Kate had a half-dozen ledgers to go over herself, so rather than lose part of their Saturday, she took the books home. They were both exhausted, under pressure, and tense about their first reunion. It could have been worse. At least they didn't fight. They'd promised not to do that. But it also could have been better. The intensity they both felt, the need to make the most of those two precious days, created a sense of unreality. They were too tense to relax; their passion was expressed not so much out of desire but out of necessity. Who knew when the next time would be?

So Kate began working more, Saturdays included, to fill space and time. She was on hold and she hated it.

The air felt stagnant as she walked down the hall to her office. She almost did an about-face as she got to her door. It was crazy to be there at nine

A.M. on a Saturday morning. It was a cold, miserable day, and she'd stayed up until two in the morning with a wicked case of insomnia. She should be curled up in bed under her nice, warm comforter. She should be curled up next to a nice, warm body belonging to one Tony Fielding. Kate let out a soft moan and unlocked her door. So much for fantasy. A half-million computer sheets beckoned. She yawned again, this time getting into it with an expansive stretching gesture.

By twelve noon she would close up shop whether she'd finished or not. She had a luncheon and shopping date with two women she'd gotten to know on her last job. Since Tony had left, Kate had begun getting together with her friends more frequently. She'd also gone out with Chris a couple of times, but their agendas were so different that their evenings together had been strained. Kate, intent on keeping the relationship purely platonic, had had to dodge all of Chris's attempts at making it into something more intimate.

She heard hollow footsteps approaching in the hall, then the rattling of the doorknob. Kate, silent and frozen, quickly thought of whom it could be: the watchman, a guard, another worker? She told herself it was foolish to be nervous, but she was all alone on the twenty-eighth floor of a nearly deserted office tower. Ever since the terrifying business with Helen Quinlan, Kate had a heightened awareness of the need for self-preservation.

Maybe whoever was lurking about out there

would go away. Kate remained frozen, trying to quell the panic clutching at her heart.

A light rap on the glass. Then stronger.

"Kate? Are you in there?"

She flew out of her seat, yanking open the door. She was in Tony's arms, breathing rapidly, face flushed, clinging to him. Relief and joy flooded her.

"Now, that's what I call a loving welcome." He grinned, then kissed her hard.

"What are you doing here?"

"I'm here to take you away from all this drudgery." He made a sweeping gesture around the room. "This is no place to be on a beautiful crisp Saturday morning."

"I had almost the same thought myself." She laughed.

"Good. Then let's get out of this place."

"How long are you here?"

"Exacty forty-five minutes, so shake a leg, beautiful."

"Hold on. Forty-five minutes?"

"Before we catch our train." He picked her pocketbook off the desk, shoved it under her arm, and started tugging her out of the office.

"Tony, what train? Where? Will you tell me what's going on?"

"I could. But then there'd be no surprise." He tilted her chin up. "I miss you."

"You do? So how come you don't look miserable?"

"I don't look miserable because for the next day and a half I intend to spend every single moment with the woman of my dreams."

"Tony, I can't just pack a bag and go off for the weekend. Why didn't you call?"

"I've been calling your house since early this morning. I couldn't call here: The switchboard is closed. So I hopped on a plane and came to get you. Now, are you going to keep wasting our precious moments by arguing?"

Kate called Thompson's Chowder House, leaving a message for her friends, and insisted Tony wait ten minutes while she finished up her work.

"I'm not good at this spur-of-the-moment stuff," she confessed, giving the office a double check before locking up. "I like to feel organized, have a sense of being on top of things."

"The change will do you good."

Kate studied him thoughtfully. It certainly seemed to be doing *him* good. But for some reason the observation didn't altogether please her.

Back at her apartment Tony tried to help her pack, but Kate couldn't stand his speedy, haphazard approach. They made it to the South Station with only five minutes to spare.

"Do I ever get to know where we're going?"

They'd settled into seats on the train, Tony sliding her case under his seat. "Katie, have I told you how much I miss you?" He put his arms around

165

her, ignoring the interested glance the couple across the aisle gave them. "Kiss me."

"Tony . . ."

"Come on. Kiss me like you've missed me. We can kiss anywhere, can't we? Who's going to stop us?"

Kate kissed him, struggling out of his grasp when he turned her brief peck into a passionate, hungry feast. "You've gone crazy," she said.

He took hold of her hands. "Things are starting to click, Katie. I've pulled off a few neat deals, and I'm working on a couple of pretty big packages now. Pete's impressed. I'm impressed." He smiled. "The travel, the excitement of negotiation, the feeling of accomplishment . . . the freedom. It's good, Kate."

"I guess you made the right decision," Kate said, a wave of depression settling in. She forced herself to smile. She should feel happy for him, right? Wrong, she admitted.

As she watched the train whip by forests speckled with white snowflakes she thought, *I'm overreacting. He was looking for self-confidence and now he's finally feeling it. I'm acting childish, selfish. He misses me. He still wants me. We're here together, aren't we?*

Tony looked out the window too. His mind traveled a very different path. The disjointed pieces of his life were beginning to fit together. The satisfaction of his new job, the ebbing paranoia, the sense

166

of family Pete and Sheila provided. Only one link was missing: Kate.

She looked pale, drained. He could tell she was working too hard, sleeping too little. He had no trouble guessing why. Their arrangement wasn't working out as smoothly as he had hoped. He wanted to see her more; even this weekend had meant an unbelievable amount of juggling, and somehow he'd have to fit a good twenty extra hours into his schedule next week. But it was worth it. If they spent much more time apart, the strain they felt when they were together would become intolerable. He still remembered the disappointment they'd felt that last time.

He had it all worked out: a cozy little room in a picturesque inn twenty miles north of Hartford, Connecticut; dinner by candlelight followed by long hours of lovemaking; breakfast in bed on Sunday; time to talk, to be together, to reconnect. He smiled to himself as Kate rested her head on his shoulder. Yes, it was going to be perfect.

The plan began falling apart as soon as they got off the train. The engine of the car Tony had rented made strange noises. It was the last rental available, so they had to hang around the dank, chilly waiting area while a mechanic tried to figure out what was the matter. Almost an hour later they were finally on the road. Kate still had no idea where they were heading.

It was at most a thirty-minute drive to the inn, but the engine, which supposedly had been cured by the garage mechanic, continued not only to knock, clank, and in general produce a veritable symphony of sounds but also prevented the car from going over twenty miles an hour. They had to get off the highway at the first exit and creep north.

The car radio was on the blink, and the heater didn't work too well, either, but Kate wasn't about to get picky. She'd settle for arriving at their mystery destination in one piece . . . and hopefully before Sunday rolled around.

Tony's ebullient spirits were rapidly declining. He scotched the surprise idea, figuring Kate deserved to know the destination of the place they might not ever get to. Every time somebody behind them beeped his horn, Tony would curse li. a truck driver, pull over so the car could pass, and then slam his fist into the steering wheel.

Kate didn't mind the cursing, but she was a little nervous about the beating that the steering wheel was receiving. With their luck it would end up in Tony's lap and they'd have to push the car to the Willow Brook Inn.

Kate grabbed his hand as he was about to smack the steering wheel for the fifth time. "Take it easy, babe. This car is temperamental enough. We wouldn't want it getting mad at us."

Tony grimaced. "Some romantic tryst. We'll probably arrive and the place will have burned down."

Kate laughed. "Relax. I'm just getting back my

spirit of adventure. It's been awhile since I needed to put it to use."

Tony rested his hand on her thigh as she snuggled closer to him. "It is a beautiful inn," he said, "providing it is still standing. I stayed there last night after working in Hartford during the day. We have a huge warehouse smack-dab in the new redevelopment district that's being converted into a combination of condominiums, offices, and a shopping mall. If we can get this car to work, I'll take you down there tomorrow and show you around. I'm hoping to close a deal on Monday with Amalgamated Insurance of New England to purchase two complete floors for their new offices. It will be my biggest coup yet."

Kate's response was less than enthusiastic, but Tony didn't seem to notice. He'd spotted the sign for the inn and his spirits immediately rose. They were only two hours off schedule.

They were both starving when they finished getting settled in their room. The dining room was empty; so was the kitchen. Lunch had ended forty minutes earlier. Tony finally tracked down Bill Clayton, the owner of the inn. The taciturn gentleman wasn't too thrilled to stop work on his boiler to fix the couple some sandwiches. He brought the food out to the small lounge, along with the news that he'd leave extra wood in their room for the fireplace because he couldn't guarantee that he'd get the boiler fixed before morning.

None of that would have mattered if Tony

hadn't received the phone call from his brother, Pete. Kate would have suffered broken engines, no heat, even hunger, as long as she and Tony were suffering through the trials and tribulations of plans gone awry together. But now Tony was telling her that he had to have his business meeting today instead of on Monday.

"I'm sorry, Kate. I just don't have any choice. Everything was worked out for Monday, but John Maddon, the guy with the power to sign the deal, is going out of town. Pete's been trying me for hours. It won't take long, I promise. Come with me and then we'll have some dinner. . . ."

She shook her head. Another hour back to Hartford in that wreck of a car and then waiting around God knew how long for Tony to conclude a business meeting didn't sound like much fun.

"You could see me in operation," he cajoled.

"We have different operations in mind," Kate muttered.

Tony smiled, his face a study in sympathy. "I had it all planned so perfectly."

"Just don't get stuck in a snowstorm and miss getting back here tonight. And I'll be careful with matches."

"I love you, Katie."

Chris shook the snow off his coat in the hallway and then handed it to Kate.

"Great weather for making snowmen. If you

170

happen to be the snowman-making type, which I'm not."

Kate smiled. "Thanks for coming over. It was short notice. I thought you'd probably have a date."

"I'm not the social whirl you're always making me out to be. Sometimes I feel old, weary, and too bored to go through the dreary routine over and over again." He gave her an affectionate squeeze. "It's nice to think about spending an evening with a lady I don't have to impress."

"You always impress me without even trying," Kate said as Chris headed for the couch, slipped off his shoes, and made himself comfortable.

She poured two glasses of wine and sat down across from him, folding her legs under her.

Chris took a sip, then peered at her over the rim of the goblet. "I hear you saw our friendly exile this past weekend."

"My, you have big ears." Kate smiled.

"I'm handling a case for Gloria Barnett. She was sorry you couldn't meet her for lunch."

"I probably should have gone with her."

"Should I pry or not?"

"Why do you think I asked you over?"

"I see."

"You sound like a lawyer."

"I am a lawyer."

"I thought you were my friend."

Kate uncoiled herself from her chair and began to pace aimlessly around the room. "I'm sorry,

Chris. Here I promised myself I would stop crying on your shoulder, and the tears are already building. It's just that . . . that everything is falling apart. Tony's sitting there in New York and you'd think he was in seventh heaven. And I'll give you three guesses where I feel like I've landed."

"He went to New York so he could feel that way, if I recall."

Kate turned to face Chris. She tugged at the turtleneck of her sweater. "I'm losing him. When we're together now, it's worse than when we're apart. Tony doesn't even see it. He thinks if he tells me he misses me enough and that he loves me, it makes everything all right. We don't have a relationship anymore; we have trysts." She said the last word with such angst, Chris had to smile.

"Come here and sit down. You're making me nervous, pacing around like that. It's what I do when I'm trying to get the jury keyed up to hand in the verdict I want."

"Do you have a verdict for me?"

Chris smiled again. "We both know the verdict, Kate. The question is the sentence. How long do you go around feeling miserable?"

"Give me my other choices."

"Do you mean it?" When she didn't answer, he sighed. "No, I didn't think so."

"I already know my options." She sat down again, her eyes on Chris. "I've been carefully considering all of them."

Chris suddenly felt nervous. For the life of him,

he couldn't say why. He was getting the first real opener from Kate . . . and he found it surprisingly unnerving. He stood up.

"What's the matter?" she asked, watching the expression on his face turn uneasy. "You look like I'm about to bite you in the neck."

"Are you?"

"I don't know," she admitted. "How would you feel about it?"

"You mean do I want to shift from unrequited love to love on the rebound?"

She grinned. "Put that way, they both sound pretty dreadful."

"Yeah, well, I'm considering my options . . . very carefully." He leaned forward, his elbows on his knees. "Something tells me we'd both be better off if we gave those considerations a little more time and thought."

"Spoken just like an attorney . . . and a good friend."

Pete was waiting up for Tony when he returned from Hartford late Sunday night. He had a couple of mugs chilling in the freezer and a six-pack of Beck's dark in the fridge. It was a night to celebrate. Tony had cinched the deal with Maddon that weekend.

Tony was surprised to find Pete sitting in the dimly lit living room at close to midnight. He was exhausted and not in the mood to recount the blow-by-blow details of his negotiations with John

Maddon. His mind wasn't on Amalgamated Insurance of New England. It was on Kate. His wonderful plans for a romantic weekend with the woman he loved had been a total bust.

He hadn't made it back to the inn by dinnertime. Kate ate her gourmet meal alone by candlelight in the quaint flower-wallpapered dining room. When Tony arrived at nine-thirty she was curled up by the fire in the reading room, fast asleep. He was all geared up. The deal had gone through. He needed that accomplishment, but it had cost him several precious hours with Kate. During what was left of the weekend he tried hard to make it up to her. By the time he put her on the train to Boston that evening he was afraid it might have cost him more than a few lost hours. Upon returning to his brother's home, he was in no mood to talk business.

Pete sensed the edge in Tony's mood.

"How about a beer?"

"No, thanks."

"I hope the short notice on the Maddon business didn't foul up your plans too much."

Tony hadn't said anything to Pete about his weekend tryst with Kate. For one thing, the whole episode had been done on impulse. For another, he was still compartmentalizing his life. Kate was in one slot, his work in another. And then there was prison, the third slot, the one he was trying to seal over. He was doing better in New York. But the nightmares still snuck into the middle of his

174

dreams. Happiness bent and twisted into torment. But he was making headway. If only the weekend had worked out according to his dreams . . .

"No problem. Maddon bit. That's the important thing, right?"

"Look, Tony, I figure I don't have to play big brother anymore. You're a grown man. You can manage your own life. Since you've been here with me and Sheila, I haven't pried; I haven't pushed you in any way to talk about anything you wanted to keep to yourself. But I don't want you to get the idea I'm not interested or concerned. You've been through one hell of a nightmare. . . ."

"You've heard me at night, huh?"

"A couple of times. Only a couple of times, Tony. Hey, it's to be expected. This buddy of mine who was in Vietnam, he still wakes up with nightmares about it."

"It's always the same. That trap, that god-awful tomb of a place. I'm walking in, the door's sealing. There's this guard looking down at me from twenty feet up, a monstrous machine gun in his hand. He's issuing orders, shouting at me, aiming. I—I can't understand what he wants me to do. I start screaming that I don't know what he's saying." A bead of sweat broke out on his brow. He wiped it with the back of his hand. "He opens fire. I keep running . . . up and down that trap . . . looking for cover . . . trying to stay alive. I can't find anyplace to hide." Tony's shoulders sagged, his hands cupping his face.

Pete put his arms around his brother. He just held him, feeling the racking sobs shudder through Tony's body. Pain wrenched at Pete's gut and tears streamed down his cheeks. He held Tony more fiercely.

After Tony calmed down, Pete shook his head in amazement. "You know," Tony said, "that's the first time I broke down since all this happened. When I was arrested and then sent to prison, I felt like I had to keep myself together or I'd go crazy. I had to hold on to my sanity the way that someone about to fall off a mountain clings to a rock. If you let go, you're a goner."

Tony sank into an armchair and took in a few deep breaths. "I feel better. Guess you still are my big brother. I'm glad."

"Me too," Pete said, then left the room for a minute, coming back with two beers and two frosty mugs.

Tony grinned. "I think I'll have that drink after all."

Pete laughed. "Nothing better than an ice-cold beer after a good cry. *I* sure as hell need it."

They were on their second round when Tony said, "Maddon did mess up my plans for the weekend."

"I had that feeling. You didn't sound too happy when I called on Saturday. A lady friend?"

Tony smiled. "More than a friend."

"I guess she wasn't too happy with my call either. You should have said something. I could have flown out."

"It was my deal, my responsibility. Anyway, the real problem goes beyond one screwed-up Saturday."

"What's the real problem?" Pete decided after that crying jag they'd shared, he could take some liberties, push a little. Tony had a tendency to hold too much inside, and he felt he needed to share it.

"The real problem is that I'm here and she's in Boston." Tony looked over at his brother. "No. The real problem is I'm still trying to figure out some way to recover from those damn nightmares. Tell me something, Pete: If I was innocent all along, even got myself an acquittal to prove it to the world, why the hell do I still feel like some kind of marked man? Not here so much. Coming to New York has been good for me—good for my morale anyway. Lousy for my love life."

"Sounds pretty serious."

"Sometimes I think she'd be better off without me. She's got this real nice guy waiting in the wings, just itching to get on stage. If I stayed out of the picture, she might give him a chance to try out for the part."

"You're too generous, little brother. I seem to remember you stepping out of the picture once before."

"I merely beat Jen to the punch. She was halfway out the door when I gave her permission to go. I'm not sorry about it."

"Well, maybe so. But it could get to be a habit. You sure this new lady is just waiting for you to give her permission to take up with the understudy?"

"I think she's waiting for me to play the part the way it's meant to be played. Only I don't know if I can do it."

CHAPTER TEN

The snow had been falling steadily since midnight. By nine in the morning the white blanket covering the city had already turned a murky gray along the roads and sidewalks. Most of the inhabitants of the city were at work or on their way there.

Kate had the day off. It wasn't a holiday. It was February fourth. Helen Quinlan's trial was one day old. Kate would have to be present for the second.

She'd taken a long time deciding on the appropriate thing to wear. This was her first court appearance. Her knowledge of proper courtroom dress came straight from prime-time TV. The women giving testimony were always costumed in the basic school-marm look. Kate finally settled on a gray tweed skirt, man-tailored white silk blouse, and dark charcoal wool blazer.

How she looked was really the least of it. Her major concern was how she felt. A few months before, the idea of giving testimony had seemed so far away. Kate hadn't given it too much thought. It was something she would do when the time came, but it wouldn't come for quite a while. And here she was, on her way to the trial. Her stomach vied with her head for first place in the pain category.

Where was Tony now when she needed him? The question had been cropping up in her mind all morning. It was four weeks since she'd seen him. Two phone calls, a postcard, and one brief letter was the sum total of their contact this whole month. And the month before, the total hadn't been that much different. After the fiasco in Connecticut, Tony had come up for New Year's weekend. At least there was one time of the year when no one was out looking for real estate investments.

They'd had a wonderful time. Tony was attentive, charming, and affectionate, and for one brief, star-burst night they'd pushed aside everything but the ecstasy of loving and being loved. Kate, like the fool she later told herself she was, thought things would actually work out. After connecting again emotionally for that one weekend, she believed they'd bridged the distance separating them.

Kate hadn't seen him since. Tony was becoming a success, which meant, of course, that he was unable to get away from work except to sleep at night. Their last phone conversation had been a disaster. Kate had confronted Tony with her firm belief that he was intentionally allowing work to absorb all of his time and energy so that he wouldn't have to think about himself, her, their relationship, and the dead-end street down which he was pushing it.

Her disheartening thoughts were interrupted when her downstairs buzzer rang. She grabbed her coat, locked up, and went to meet Chris Coleman in the lobby. He would be testifying today as well.

"You look less confident as a witness than you do as an attorney," Kate said as she greeted him.

"I was hoping I looked better than I felt. You've shot that one down."

"Well, don't feel bad. I look worse than you."

"For some reason that doesn't help. I definitely prefer being on the asking rather than the answering side of a stand."

"This will give you humility." Kate grinned.

"Or indigestion."

In the cab ride to the courthouse, Kate drummed her fingers on her black leather purse until Chris finally put his hand over hers. "You're going to wear out your nails. Take it easy."

"I'm a star witness. I've got reason to be nervous. I keep thinking about Helen Quinlan. Until this happened, she was hardly more than a voice on the phone to me. Most of the time I dealt with Todd Nichols. For a while there, I had him down as a prime suspect. But Helen . . . she was so quiet, so nondescript. She looked so . . . so innocent."

"So did Ma Barker, I hear tell."

Kate sighed. Chris put his arm around her. He had been sure that Tony would come to be with Kate during this ordeal. Tony had almost been served a subpoena to testify. For a time Ron Delaney had considered calling Tony in for testimony, but since all of Tony's evidence would be labeled hearsay, he'd decided against it.

Chris knew how tough this experience was for Kate. She had a tender heart. She didn't want to see anyone suffer, even someone like Helen Quinlan, who Kate knew was guilty of embezzlement—embezzlement that had landed Tony Fielding in jail for fourteen months and could have landed Kate there as well.

As far as her near-miss with the Triumph was concerned, Kate had all but convinced herself that Helen had really meant only to scare her. Ron Delaney, the prosecuting attorney, had argued with Kate for hours about not presenting her opinions to the jury, just the facts.

Chris knew from an attorney's perspective that Kate was a lousy witness. It was not going to be easy to convince the jury to bring in a guilty verdict on an attempted-murder charge. Ron was a pretty effective jury lawyer, though, and he might manage to get Quinlan on an attempted-assault charge.

Chris thought he could tell when Kate was thinking about Tony. Like right now. She'd gone from finger-drumming to that slightly vacant, faraway stare. All the way to New York. Chris skimmed a finger along her cheek. She turned to him and smiled; the distant look faded.

Tony was there. Chris was here. For the past few weeks he was trying to take as much advantage of that fact as possible. But he was careful about not coming on too strong, too quickly. He'd gotten over his initial jitters about Kate, but he knew better than to assume it was more than just a glimmer of hope she offered him. Kate still thought that she and Tony would somehow work things out. She'd even mentioned she might have made the wrong decision about not going to New York with him.

But Kate's job was going too well for Chris to get overly worried about her pulling up stakes. She loved the work, the status, the sense of making it in a tough profession. He could see the pride she took in her success. It was all very low-key, but Chris knew her well enough to know Kate was a woman who liked to win. She saw things through to the end. Wasn't that the reason she was sitting beside him in this cab on the way to the courthouse? Wasn't it also the reason she still kept her hopes alive where Tony Fielding was concerned?

When she was sworn in, Kate's "I do" sounded oddly unlike her real voice. The words seemed so strikingly misplaced. She'd hoped to say those words at her wedding. Instead she was sitting in this alien place, swearing to tell the truth, the whole truth, and nothing but the truth. She glanced down at her hands and saw that they were trembling. She was so out of touch that she didn't even realize it until she looked.

She focused on the questions. The facts were fairly simple to recount. She described clearly, concisely, how she began picking up errors, kept checking deeper, started putting two and two together. Telling the facts had a calming effect. It wasn't going to be as difficult as she thought.

And then Helen's attorney, Bill Wallaston, began his interrogation. At first Kate's knowledge of the facts kept her poised. She repeated her findings, detailing the way the double entries had been worked along with the fictitious transactions to pull money out of the company slowly. As long as it was done intermittently and in small amounts, the money could be sifted out through wire transfers. Until a full audit of the books at the end of a fiscal year, the withdrawals could easily go undetected. Even when the truth became clear, clever manipulations could cast blame on an innocent party.

"Like Mr. Anthony Fielding, former employee at Howell and Beck, who had previously been charged and found guilty of embezzlement at the same company?"

"And acquitted of all charges," she said, her voice rising, sounding more like her own.

"Please answer the question, Miss Stuart."

"Yes," she said softly.

"Do you know Mr. Fielding?"

"Yes."

"Could you tell us what your relationship is to Mr. Fielding?"

Kate hesitated for a moment, glancing over at Ron Delaney. He had warned her that Wallaston would try to discredit her as an expert witness any way he could. The evidence against Helen Quinlan was strong enough so that her only real defense was to question the expertise and character of each of the witnesses for the prosecution. Kate fixed her gaze back on Wallaston. "Mr. Fielding is a good friend of mine."

" 'A good friend'?" He accented the *good,* casting a look at the jury. "A good friend, I believe, whom you met while he was in prison."

"Yes."

"Could you tell the jury why you initially went to visit Mr. Fielding in prison?"

"I . . . discovered a series of errors on several computer transaction forms. I wanted to discuss them with Mr. Fielding." *Keep the answers brief—* Ron had drummed that into her head. *Don't ever give Wallaston more than he absolutely asks for.*

Wallaston shook his head for a moment, an expression of confusion on his face—an expression that, Kate felt certain, was a ploy. Wallaston was just warming up.

"That's very interesting, Miss Stuart. But I'm confused. You begin to suspect someone might be embezzling funds from the company, so you go seek out another embezzler to discuss your findings with?"

"It has been established, Mr. Wallaston, that Mr. Fielding is not an embezzler. He is an innocent man, wrongly accused and acquitted. Helen

185

Quinlan altered the editing reports to make it look—"

Wallaston, frowning, broke in. "Please stick to the question at hand, Miss Stuart. You are not being asked your opinions of who did what right now. To get back . . ." He wiped his brow. "When you first went to see Mr. Fielding, you did not know he was innocent. Correct?"

Kate took a deep breath. She placed her hands in her lap, trying to remain calm. Ron had not only been accurate about Bill Wallaston, Kate had completely underestimated the reaction she would have to his line of questioning. Feeling her heartbeat pounding in her ears, she fought to stay poised. "I did not know Mr. Fielding was innocent at the time. However—"

Again he cut her off. He only wanted her rambling if it would benefit his client. "Why, then, did you choose to discuss these matters with a man who, as you admit, was considered a felon, a clever embezzler in his own right?"

"Wouldn't you go to an expert, Mr. Wallaston, if you wanted information about a particular topic? Who better to understand what was going on . . . ?"

Titters in the courtroom. Kate smiled pleasantly at Wallaston, whose annoyance was well masked. Helen Quinlan hadn't gotten herself a hack. He smiled back.

"It's also possible that you'd heard a great deal of talk at the company about Mr. Fielding. Quite a romantic figure, don't you think? Nice young fellow, quite a good-looking man. Perhaps you saw a picture or received some descriptions of him from a few of the women employees."

"I . . . knew a little about Mr. Fielding. People did not discuss the case very much, though."

"I see. Yet, knowing so little you sought him out . . . because of your suspicions. He must have found that somewhat odd."

Kate flashed back to that first meeting with Tony. She'd tried to explain it all to him that day. She remembered his distrust, his hostility, the very same questions she was now being asked. She also remembered her initial attraction, an attraction that had developed into something so much deeper.

"He was surprised at my meeting with him."

"Pleasantly surprised, no doubt."

Kate felt herself flush, but she was irritated at the same time. "I'm not the one who can answer that."

"Come, now, Miss Stuart. You have already stated that you and Mr. Fielding are 'good friends.' Isn't it true that you are more than friends, Miss Stuart? In fact, isn't it true that you were quite attracted to Mr. Fielding when you first met him—so attracted that you made up your mind that you would do anything to prove his innocence?"

"No. No. That's not the way—"

"Weren't you already infatuated with the man

from what you'd learned about him at your office? Were you romanticizing about this very attractive man wasting away in a prison cell, a man who proclaimed his innocence? Had you perhaps begun building up a fantasy before you even met—a romantic notion about rescuing a handsome innocent man? I must say, it's a novel approach to finding a boyfriend."

Kate kept shaking her head, unable to get a word in, but Bill Wallaston wasn't giving her any opportunity.

"I object, Your Honor. The counselor is using innuendo and making uncalled-for suppositions," Ron shouted.

"Objection sustained. Please save your conclusions for the summation, Mr. Wallaston."

"Yes, Your Honor." He turned to Kate and smiled, pressing his palms together.

Kate looked over at the judge. "I would like to explain to the court why I went to see Mr. Fielding in prison." She could tell, glancing at Ron, that he wasn't pleased, but Kate was adamant about not letting Wallaston drop his line of questioning with her own character still impugned.

The judge nodded.

"After picking up some unusual but seemingly innocuous errors, I discovered several transaction forms bearing my initials. However, I had never seen these forms before, nor had I signed them. It became very clear that whoever was manipulating funds could be trying to set me up. At that time I thought what was happening to me might well have happened to Mr. Fielding. He'd always maintained his innocence, and none of the money had been found.

"My first objective in talking with Mr. Fielding was that I wanted to do everything I could to protect myself. I was not about to sit back and let somebody set me up and send me to jail. I thought that if Mr. Fielding was indeed innocent, as he had claimed, he would have some feeling for my predicament and help me as well as himself to try to uncover the truth.

"Mr. Wallaston, here, seems intent on implying something tawdry about my relationship with Mr. Fielding. It wasn't any schoolgirl rescue fantasy that brought me to Anthony Fielding. It was a purely selfish decision on my part to get all the help I could to make sure what happened to him didn't happen to me. It is true that when the evidence I was finding pointed more clearly to the fact that Tony—Mr. Fielding—was innocent, I did want to help him if I could. I also had a responsibility to my company. I certainly could not sit back and let embezzlement occur right under my nose, or let an innocent man suffer more than he already had. What kind of a person could do that? I suppose only somebody who was so intent on a criminal path that she would let somebody else pay the price.

"My experience in helping Mr. Fielding did bring us close together, as I've already admitted.

But our relationship, despite what Mr. Wallaston has implied, had nothing to do with fantasy. It was based on reality. It was based on respect, caring, and sympathy for a man suffering an unjust punishment, who still bears the pain of that suffering to this day." Her eyes filled with tears, and she looked away from the jury to the rear of the courtroom. And that's when she saw him.

Tony was sitting in the last row. She had no idea how long he'd been there. She'd been so caught up in her emotional outpouring that she hadn't seen him come in. But he was there now. A wave of relief washed over her. She was still trembling, but she knew now she'd be all right.

When Wallaston quickly shifted to the alleged hit-and-run attempt, Kate was calmer, more composed. He couldn't shake her testimony that she definitely did recognize Helen Quinlan behind the wheel of that car.

Wallaston, concluding that the jury was strongly sympathetic to the impassioned young woman, came to the quick decision that the best thing he could do for his client was to get Kate Stuart off the stand. She had created too much emotion and interest.

"I have no more questions, Your Honor." He glared briefly at Kate and then sat down.

Kate's legs felt weak as she stood up. She grabbed tightly to the wooden rail as she paused to get her equilibrium. She met Tony's gaze. He stepped into the aisle and waited for her. Kate smiled, lifted her head, and walked toward him. Together they left the courtroom.

Chris Coleman was being sworn in. He put his left hand over the Bible, raised his right hand, said "I do," and took his place on the witness stand. The whole time his eyes watched the couple walking out the door, arm in arm.

Walking into the courtroom that morning had not been an easy task for Tony. It had a painful quality of déjà-vu. Kate was just beginning her testimony. He knew she hadn't seen him come in. He sat down in the last row.

It was all so similar—the setting, the words, the rhythm of justice being done. Only he wasn't the one sitting up front this time, on trial. On trial. The memories flooded back, Kate's voice fading as he once again heard the witnesses for his own defense.

His lawyer had told him he stood a good chance. All the evidence against him was circumstantial. The problem was, it amounted to a hell of a lot of circumstance. Was he a cunning criminal, clever enough to set himself up intentionally as a poor boob being used as a scapegoat—an embezzler who lacked the brains to conceal his wrongdoing—or an innocent victim?

Guilty. Guilty as charged. The words swirled around his brain. Tony broke into a sweat. He gripped the chair in front of him. For a moment he considered fleeing. This was what he was afraid of, why he almost didn't show up at all. Could he stave off the pain, the panic, the past that was still chasing him in the dark?

And then Kate's voice came back into focus—forceful, determined, intense. He looked up at her. She was nearly in tears, but she kept on talking. He began to concentrate on her words, then more significantly on the love her words conveyed.

The past receded. He watched Kate walk toward him. He stepped forward to meet her. With his arm around her waist he felt her shiver. He held her tighter and got her out of there. In the hallway they embraced in silence for several moments. Then Kate whispered, "It means so much to me to have you here. So much." She kissed him deeply, gratefully. She kept her arm around his waist as he gently steered her to the stairs.

"Come on, baby, let's get out of here." He pulled her closer to him, then took her hand from his waist, holding it tightly, securely.

In the cab she leaned on his shoulder, his arm cradling her. When they reached her apartment, Tony paid the driver, scooted around to Kate's side of the cab, and helped her out. The snow had tapered off, but the path, shoveled earlier, had received another thick dusting. They walked carefully up the walk, first Kate nearly slipping, then Tony. They laughed. The sound felt good to both of them.

"God, I'm glad to see you." Kate smiled. "I kept telling myself it wasn't fair to go on hoping you'd come. I know how hard it must have been for you to relive—"

Tony silenced her with a kiss. Then he looked at her warmly. "I could have used you for my defense back then. You'd have made an unforgettable witness."

Kate grinned. "That Wallaston is an insulting idiot."

"He's just a lawyer trying to save his client's skin."

"I know."

Once inside Kate's apartment, neither of them was interested in rehashing the morning's experience. Kate immediately went into the bedroom to change out of her courtroom outfit. When she walked back into the living room, she was smiling, the pallor gone from her complexion. She was wearing a soft blue challis robe and a very provocative expression.

Tony laughed softly, stretching out his arms to her. She came to him, perched herself on his lap, and sighed as he slipped one hand inside the opening of her robe.

"Nice," she whispered. "You have such a nice touch."

She inclined her head to look more directly at him. He cupped her chin, kissed her lips lightly, then whispered her name, kissing her once more.

Kate returned his kisses tenfold, greedy for him, sharply aware of just how much she'd missed him all those weeks. She wanted him desperately. It went beyond a fierce physical need, although that was certainly there. It was more a sense that without him she did not feel complete. She took his hand, leading him to the bedroom, undressing him like the rare treasure he was.

He caught her in his arms, falling with her onto the bed, his strong hands clasping her. Kate flung one leg over his hip, pinning him to her more securely. He removed a hand from beneath her back to trace the curves of her body. Languidly, determined to make the most of these few precious stolen moments together, Tony caressed her, kissing, touching, gazing.

Kate cried out for him. His embraces made her reel. He ran his tongue over her nipples, then down the well-marked line of her rib cage to her navel. She clung to him, her breathing rapid, her hands kneading, clawing, grasping on to him. She could feel the ripple of his muscles as she ran her hands over his firm, hard body, his weight fully on her.

She was poised on a thin, jagged precipice as he suddenly lunged inside of her, sending her careening out of control. Falling through that dark, warm void of pure sensation, unconscious of time, flung about in space, abandoning all but the feeling, so pure, so intense. Her body pulsated with his, throbbing, contracting, wild, free. Shuddering with release, Kate cried out his name over and over.

Then together they rocked back and forth, their

bodies moist, clinging, not wanting to relinquish the moment. He nestled his face in her hair, slipping off her at last when he was afraid he was crushing her. But she was smiling: His weight was a joy, not a burden. She massaged his shoulders and neck, slipping her fingers through his hair, pulling him closer for another kiss—a loud smacking kiss, satisfied, content, fulfilled.

Tony laughed, kissing her back with equal gusto.

"Why don't we do this more often?" She grinned, then laid her cheek in the hollow of his neck, not wanting to risk seeing the answer reflected in his features. Not now. She was too happy. *Let this moment be. Don't tamper with it. Don't damage it with reminders of partings, long weeks alone again, fears, doubts.* Today he was hers, all hers. A circle complete.

Tony lay back on the pillows, eyes closed.

"You must have gotten up at the crack of dawn to get here," she said softly.

"Before the crack of dawn by a good hour." He opened his eyes. "Then I spent two hours working up the courage to walk back into that courtroom. I didn't call to tell you I would be there because, to be honest, I wasn't sure I could handle it."

"But you did."

"Thanks to you."

"What did I do?"

He smiled, touching her cheek tenderly. "You made the present more alive, more significant, than the past for me."

195

"I want that to be true not just for today. I hate the separation."

He sat up, his eyes meeting hers. "Katie, come to New York with me. I'm doing better every day. I'm making a new life for myself, but I—I need you."

"Then come home. You faced your past today. Why not—?"

"No. I can't."

"Then things aren't any better. Don't you see, Tony? You're not dealing with the past. You've just continued to avoid it. It's not a new life you've created; it's a cover."

"I don't agree," he said defensively. "I think you just want it all your own way. When it comes to making the choice between your career and the man you're supposedly in love with, the fact is, you always choose the former."

"You make it sound like the choice is put before me every day," she countered, then caught herself before she flew off the handle. "Oh, Tony, I don't want to hide under a cover with you. I don't want to have to flee to a new city, find a new job, create a new life, when the only thing keeping you from coming back here is a sense of shame that it enrages me to think you have to suffer! Can't you see that it's robbing you of your right to feel whole and free?" Exasperated, she added, "You're still a prisoner. Only now *you*'re the one turning the key."

He shook his head sadly. "It's always the same

stalemate." His eyes rested on her. "It's not just shame, Kate. It's the bitterness, the resentment, that crowds me in here. I don't feel like I'm a freak in New York. For now, I'll settle for that." He got out of bed and dressed. "I've got to get back for a dinner meeting."

Kate watched him, struggling with her conscience. Was there truth in Tony's accusation? Was she choosing her career over him? Did she simply want things her own way? Had she always? Was it selfishness or a real sense that what Tony was doing was the wrong thing, an injustice he was committing against himself?

He looked over at her. "I'll admit one thing: This commuting arrangement isn't working out at all. I love you, Katie. I want you to change your mind. Think about it, okay?"

"Ditto," she said softly, watching him walk out the door.

CHAPTER ELEVEN

Kate smiled across the boardroom table at Laura Gladstone. "Why is it that the men clear out of these meetings faster than we do?"

"So they can get down to the clubroom, light their smelly cigars, and talk 'man talk,'" Laura said with a broad grin. "So, what do you say we go get ourselves some lunch and talk 'woman talk'?"

"I think we should crash the clubroom and find out what our esteemed colleagues are really like behind closed doors," Kate declared. "But, on second thought, I'd probably be bored stiff. Lunch sounds great."

Laura Gladstone turned out to be a food connoisseur who knew about every restaurant worth knowing within a ten-block radius. After asking Kate where she'd like to go, Laura, in typical fashion, ended up not only selecting the place but put in a strong pitch for what Kate should order.

"Now you know why I've got where I am at Howell and Beck. I'm a pushy broad," she said with a chuckle. "Don't think I don't know I'm called Bulldozer. Affectionately, of course," she quipped.

Kate laughed. She liked Laura Gladstone in spite of her "bulldozer" style. Laura was wise enough to know you get nothing in this world without being aggressive, and you make friends along the way if you can laugh at yourself a little as you're climbing upward.

"So, go ahead. Have the lamb chops instead of the steak au poivre," Laura said. "We all have to learn from our own mistakes."

Kate smiled. "A lesson I am learning every day." She gave the waitress her order: lamb chops, broiled rare, with a small tossed salad.

Laura instructed the waitress in detail on how she wanted her steak prepared, that she did not want to see a hint of tin foil around her baked potato, and if her string beans were not al dente, forget them and bring a salad—no spinach or onions; olive oil and red wine vinegar on the side.

The waitress was a great study in restrained contempt. Once she saw what she was up against, she plastered a smile on her lips, but she was having trouble keeping the rest of her face in line. Her eyes continued narrowing with each additional instruction, so that by the time Laura Gladstone was through with her, the waitress's eyes were two small slits, the phony smile wilted to a grimace.

"I make up for my obnoxious behavior by being a big tipper. Did I embarrass you?" Laura asked in her cavalier fashion.

"No. I love seeing you in operation . . . at a restaurant or in the boardroom. I'm learning quite a lot from you. You keep everyone hopping all the time. They never know what curveball you are going to throw next."

"If you're in the position to throw the ball, always put a spin on it, Kate. That way you stand a better chance of the other guy striking out. You're throwing some good ones. I've been watching you carefully. Had to make sure you were no flash in the pan." She grinned. "I admit I was as impressed as the next guy when you discovered Helen Quinlan was dipping her sticky fingers into the till. You're a smart girl and you've got guts."

"Thanks, but I might never have discovered it was Helen doing the dipping if she hadn't almost dipped into me that day. It allowed the final pieces of the puzzle to come together."

"Lucky for you, you were still standing to fit them into place. Lucky for my friend Tony Fielding as well."

Kate looked more closely at Laura. "I didn't realize you and Tony are friends."

"Past tense. Since you sprang him, we haven't been what you'd call buddy-buddy. I don't really blame him, although I did try to stay in touch. I guess it sounds like I'm tooting my horn now that everything's been resolved, but I never believed Tony Fielding was guilty for one minute. I tried to work on Howell, Beck, the guy from the FBI in charge of the case, and Jim Holderness, who was chief accountant back then. I honestly did go to bat for the guy. You know where it got me? I wrote Tony a few times, but what the hell do you say in a letter to a man in prison? I felt guilty writing good news. He sure didn't need to hear the bad stuff, given his miserable existence. They were pathetic, empty letters."

"At least you wrote."

"How is he doing in New York? Are the two of you still seeing each other?"

"We get together on rare occasions. I've met him in New York a few times. Tony tries to get up here once every two or three weeks. He says he's doing well, but lately we don't see eye to eye on many issues. If you want my opinion, I think he's still fighting shadows."

"He's a very sensitive guy. Few people realized that way back when he was your typical preppy-looking investment broker. To see him then, you'd have sworn he fit in perfectly. But I always had the feeling some of the edges didn't quite set in to place. Almost like he was trying too hard. He was so damn earnest—worked his butt off for the company—and look where it got him. Jeez, that must have killed him. It tore right through me, thinking about what was happening to him. The last time I saw Tony—in that courtroom, being sentenced— he looked so forlorn and defeated. How do you learn to trust, to pick up the pieces after that? It isn't easy."

"But if you can't pick up the pieces, if you sweep

them under the rug, how do you ever start living your life again?" Kate could hear the bitter edge to her voice. It came from her own sense of defeat. With each passing week she and Tony grew further apart.

Neither of them had maintained their stand-offish positions. It was too scary. They knew each other well enough to know neither would move off the mark. And they weren't ready to call it quits, despite all the arguments, the tension, the stale-mates. So the Eastern shuttle was still making money off them, although not too much.

Kate hated the pattern she and Tony were set-tling into, and she knew he didn't like it either. They worked hard to accept the situation, and reached out to each other with formality so they wouldn't spoil their time together. But the stress continued to take its toll. The traveling was bad enough, but what was more grueling was the strain of behaving contrary to their feelings. Kate some-times thought that it might be better if they went back to fighting all the time—anything to disrupt the carefully constructed front. She was always the one championing confrontation and facing harsh realities. Tony held to the firm belief that he'd had enough harsh realities to confront for fourteen months of his life and he deserved a break.

Laura Gladstone, contrary to her projected im-age, had a sensitive, understanding nature that she obviously chose not to display too often. Kate was grateful to see it this afternoon.

"It's tough when you're the one at bat and the guy you happen to care about is throwing the curves. But hang in there, sweetie. You look like the type who can hit a home run if you keep swinging." Laura broke into one of her infectious chuckles. "Will you listen to me? We're supposed to be talking girl talk and I'm gabbing batting averages. Before you came up to the twenty-eighth floor, I was stuck listening to so much baseball talk that I actually got turned on to the game. I become downright nasty when anyone puts down the Red Sox nowadays."

"I happen to be a tried-and-true Red Sox fan myself," Kate said.

They eventually got around to the girl talk when Laura settled down to her steak au poivre, and Kate ate her overdone lamp chops, admitting she should have listened to Laura after all.

Chris Coleman stood outside Kate's apartment door, trying to revive the frostbitten bouquet of flowers he was carrying. They'd just come through the latest snowstorm in this record-breaking winter of blizzards. Finally giving up on the flowers, he knocked on the door.

Kate was on the phone with Tony. She asked him to hold on while she went to get the door, but he told her he was feeling rotten and wanted to get back in bed, so he hung up.

Scratch another weekend, she thought, irritated and depressed. Her life seemed to be moving ahead on a straight path, but she felt as if she were merely tagging along after it. For a woman who liked order and control, she was, in Laura's unique brand of talk, batting zero. Double zero. Saturday and Sunday shot.

Chris, standing at the door, glanced from a glum-looking Kate to the limp clump of hothouse irises in his fist. He had a feeling he should have seen the demise of the bouquet as a definite omen.

Kate looked at the flowers, a smile, weak but present, altering the tight grimace. "They're . . . they're . . ."

"They're dead," Chris said, the grimace contagious. He walked inside, headed for the kitchen, and dumped the bouquet into the trash. "It was a dumb idea anyway."

"You're in as bad a mood as I am," she said.

"That must mean we're meant for each other," he said dryly.

"Tony's not coming in this weekend. He's sick in bed and had to reschedule some meetings . . . damn it. He does these things so often, you'd think I'd get used to it."

"Or get fed up."

Kate eyed him sharply. "It's not his fault that he got a cold."

"Give me a break, Kate. I liked it better when you were honest and got teed off at how Tony was dealing with you. Now you've taken to making excuses every time the guy stands you up."

"I'm not making excuses. I'm miserable. You

204

should know that better than anyone. I've bent your ear enough times with my woes."

"You're right."

"Have I used up my quota?"

"I'm running out of mine. My shoulder can take only so much absorption."

"I can understand that," she said softly.

Chris sighed. "Can you? I wonder."

They'd gotten to this spot before. Kate walked over to the closet for her coat. "We'd better get going, Chris. I made an eight-o'clock reservation for dinner—a nice, fun dinner with a friend, remember?" she teased. Only Chris wasn't in the mood to be sidetracked tonight. He was tired of being the "friend," a shoulder to cry on, the guy on the losing end of a triangle.

"Forget the dinner."

"Come on, Chris."

"No, Kate. None of your fancy maneuvers this time to keep the conversation from starting."

Kate stood poised at the closet, her hand gripping her jacket. She finally let go and turned around to face Chris.

"I know how you feel. And you know how I feel. So what's the point of going through this?"

"The point is, I'm tired of playing the part of odd guy out. I keep trying to find a way in and you keep slamming the door in my face. Pretty soon you're going to have to pay for a nose job." He walked over to Kate and put his hands lightly on her shoulders, his dark brown eyes meeting hers

205

squarely. "Kate, at least let me get my foot in the door."

"Chris," she took a step back, "you're a good friend."

"I'm an even better lover. If you'd give me half a chance, you might find that out for yourself."

"Tony and I—"

"Tony and you have had more grief than half the couples that walk into my office, looking for a divorce. The two of you are locked in a no-win situation." He moved toward her again, and Kate's back was already at the wall, so she had no place to go. "I'm in love with you, Kate, and I have been for years. I know I don't have the greatest track record for relationships, but this is different. And don't start giving me the argument that it's only the challenge I'm after."

Kate smiled as Chris took hold of her hands. "It's an argument I happen to believe."

"Give me the opportunity to prove you wrong." His voice was husky. He was standing so close that Kate's breath ruffled his hair, causing his grip on her hands to tighten.

Kate felt her breath catch as Chris leaned toward her, his lips meeting hers. She had the craziest sensation: Part of her was lost to the intensity of his kiss, while another part hovered over, watching, questioning—worst of all, comparing. Her body stiffened. Chris froze along with her, drawing away.

His feelings were hurt. Kate saw the faint flush

rising in his neck and moving up over his jawline. She found herself wishing she could have let go completely. Chris was attractive, appealing, certainly intent on winning her over. She cared for him. It wasn't love, but Chris wouldn't expect that . . . yet. He wanted a chance. Kate's problem was that she wanted Tony.

Chris was reaching for her coat. He stood at the closet, waiting to help her into it. Kate smiled wistfully. "I'm sorry, Chris."

"I had you there for a moment." He walked back to her and stroked her cheek. He wanted to kiss her again, but instead he slipped her coat around her shoulders, settling for the sisterly peck she planted on his cheek.

"You had me there for a moment." She grinned.

The tension melted with their laughter.

"Oh, before I forget," Chris said, still smiling at her, "Helen Quinlan was found guilty of attempted assault and embezzlement. They sentenced her to five years. I know you were upset about her, Kate, but believe me, she got what she deserved, and it could have been a lot worse."

Kate nodded. "I guess you're right, but I can't help feeling sorry for that poor woman."

"I know," Chris answered. "Hey, I just got this terrific idea. It should take your mind off all this bad news," Chris said, trying to sound casual and very spur of the moment.

Kate gave him a wry smile. "Oh?"

"You've suddenly got the whole weekend free

and I just happen to be going to a Saturday-morning seminar up in Montreal. Why don't we go together? You can shop and sightsee while I take care of business, and then we'd have the weekend to—Get that suspicious look out of your eye! I was about to suggest that we take a suite. The Hyatt has some terrific ones with great views of the city. Connecting doors between the bedrooms that lock from both sides." He smiled. "There was that moment, Kate. Maybe there are more in store for us, if you'll give it a chance to happen. What do we have to lose? At the worst, we'll have some great French Canadian meals, take in a club or two, and you can pick up some terrific bargains in English wool. Nothing has to happen that you don't want to happen."

"I don't think it's a good idea."

"Why not?"

Kate was stumped for an answer. Why not? She was scared, that was why not. She was in love with Tony Fielding. Another *why not:* She was far too vulnerable, lonely, confused. Montreal sounded too appealing. Chris's kiss had not left her cold. She didn't need more complications in her life. And she didn't want to ruin a good friendship. There were a wealth of *why nots.* So how come she was standing there, staring at Chris, at a loss for words? Because in the midst of all those perceptive, logical, intelligent reasons for turning him down flat, Kate felt tempted. Tempted enough not to throw the list of *why nots* in his face.

"No demands?" was all she said.

Chris nodded, hand raised in the air, boy-scout fashion.

"Chances are extremely good that the lock is going to stay bolted on my side," Kate said.

"Understood."

"Are you sure about this, Chris? You could find any number of women to take to Montreal who'd be thrilled to share one bedroom. Think of all the money you'd save."

"I write these trips off."

"If Tony hadn't canceled out on this weekend, I'd never have considered your offer," she told him bluntly.

"I know. And I know this trip could be a bust. I know that you're probably going to put a chair against your door as well as lock it. I know that I'm moving in on the rebound. I know I want you to come with me. Will you?"

"Yes. As long as we have a clear understanding, I'll go," she said in her most formal, controlled voice. As if somehow that would set the tone for the weekend and save her from making a potentially whopping mistake.

The tissue box was empty. Tony groaned, threw back the covers, and eased himself out of bed. Every muscle in his body hurt. His pajamas clung to him. His head was spinning. And he was about to sneeze again.

He got to an unopened box of tissues in the

bathroom as his sneeze erupted. Leaning against the sink, he mangled the perforated top, getting the box open as the next sneeze escaped. When he caught a glance at himself in the mirror, he felt even worse. He hadn't looked this bad since . . . prison.

The image never did go away. It was held fast in his mind's eye, popping into clear view unbidden, catching him off guard, the rage and despair surfacing again. He slammed the box of tissues onto the hamper. Then he picked them up again, remembering that that was what had brought him in there in the first place.

He climbed back into bed. When he'd called Kate a few minutes earlier, he'd told her he felt too rotten to talk. He'd also felt guilty about canceling out on the weekend. And disappointed. As disappointed as she was, but he knew she didn't believe him.

He picked up the phone to call her back. He could feel her slipping away, and the thought terrified him. He loved her. She was the one fine, pure, tender part of his life. A soft caress against the rough texture of his existence. He couldn't lose her.

He let the phone ring a dozen times. She was out. She'd told him she was going to dinner with Chris. Tony leaned back against the pillow, the receiver still in his hand, the droning ring drifting into the air. Shrugging in resignation, he placed it back on its cradle.

When he heard the light rapping on his door, he considered pretending to be asleep. But whether it was the flu or his silent fears, Tony found his defenses down. He was tired of pretenses, tired of trying to wipe out fourteen months of his life as if they had never existed.

Pete walked into the room at Tony's invitation.

"How are you feeling?" he asked.

"Lousy."

"I'd better warn you, Sheila's down in the kitchen, boiling up some more soup. Chicken with rice this time. I'm supposed to be up here, tactfully trying to discover whether that was another prison favorite. So, was it?"

Tony grinned. "That was tactful. I gather you told her about the tomato soup."

"You mad?"

"No," he said.

"I just thought . . . well, you certainly never bring up the subject."

"It hurts, that's why." Tony studied his brother's face for several moments. "I was terrified when they first brought me through that trap. I said to myself, *You're not going to make it, fellow.* But what choice did I have? You make it because the days go by, you fall into a routine, you even start thinking to yourself, *It's not that bad.* The real world stops existing. There's this little microcosm of life that becomes the only reality. Only it isn't real. The whole time, a part of my mind kept

211

saying, *This is madness. This isn't you in that locked room, behind those concrete walls.*"

Tony's eyes looked past his brother to other visions. "It was a black-and-white world, right down to the clothes. Like somebody had come along and snatched the color out of my life. Just up and stole it right out from under me. I walked around in a fog for months on end. That's the way I wanted it. It was the only way I could endure the monotony, the isolation, the complete loss of identity.

"Then one day I walked into the visitors' room and the fog got blown away in one incredible storm. There's this woman sitting there . . . incredibly beautiful, vibrant, so alive and spirited, I fell in love with her on the spot. The kind of love you feel when you see a fabulous-looking actress prancing across your TV screen and you're lying alone in your cot behind that locked door. Only Kate was real. She kept coming back to see me."

Pete knew a little about Kate. While Tony was still in prison, he'd written to his older brother that a woman at Howell and Beck was uncovering evidence that could lead to his acquittal. But Tony had said little about his personal relationship with Kate. Pete didn't have any trouble figuring out that she was the woman he was seeing in Boston, but until now he didn't realize the intensity of his brother's feelings for her. Or how strong Kate's feelings must be for Tony.

"She sounds like a very special lady. Not one that comes along every day," Pete said, treading

212

lightly. He didn't want to scare Tony away from opening up. It happened so rarely.

"She's very strong, determined. Successful too. A woman who knows what she wants, goes after it, gets it. What does she need a guy like me for?"

"What are you talking about? Listen to me, Tony. You are your own worst enemy. Do you know that? You're a bright, sensitive guy who's been to hell and back. The journey isn't without its problems. No big surprise. You're beginning to open up. That's good—real good. The thing to do now is to stop selling yourself short. You're not the only man to have suffered an injustice. Sure, it leaves scars. But from what you tell me about Kate, it sounds like she can handle a few scars. Especially if you're not spending half the time covering them up."

Tony smiled. "The two of you would hit it off."

"Good. Bring her around."

Sheila stood at the door to Tony's room, holding a bowl of soup.

"Hey, Sheila. Is that chicken-and-rice soup I smell? How did you know that was the one soup I dreamed of having the whole fourteen months I was in the slammer?"

Pete and Tony broke up laughing. Sheila stared at the two of them as if they'd both gone crazy. For a man with the flu, Tony hadn't felt so good in a long time.

After Sheila and Pete left, he rang Kate up again. Still no answer. That was an awfully long

213

dinner. Tony made up his mind to cancel his Sunday meeting and go to Boston for the day. He had no clearer idea about a resolution to the problems he was having with Kate, but he knew one thing: He wanted to keep working with her on solutions.

CHAPTER TWELVE

Kate could hear the phone ringing as she was unlocking her door. Naturally, as soon as she got
inside, it stopped. She took off her coat, tossed it
over a chair, started to walk into her bedroom,
then turned back, lifting the coat and hanging it up
neatly in the closet. Her need for order prevailed in
the midst of confusion and doubt.

Why had she told Chris she would go with him
to Montreal? She'd spent the whole evening at the
El Diablo Restaurant trying to talk her way out of
it. Chris wasn't about to let her off the hook, effectively countering all of her rationalizations for why
it wasn't going to work. By the time they left the
restaurant, Kate had run out of arguments and
Chris, now that his foot was in the door, was just
brimming with determination. He wisely left her at
the entrance to her apartment building so that if
she came up with some new excuse, she wouldn't
be able to lay it on him.

Kate was slipping her nightgown over her head
when the phone started to ring again. She hesitated
for a brief moment, guessing it must be Tony. A

flash of guilt washed over her. He was probably calling to apologize again about the weekend. Well, she had certainly made sure she wouldn't be spending those two days pining away.

She reached for the receiver on the fifth ring.

"Oh, Kate. Am I glad I got you in."

"Laura? What's the matter?"

"Remember your offer the other day to let me stay for a few days at your place while I was having my kitchen redone?"

"The offer is still open."

"Good. Because the firemen are just leaving my building now."

"Oh, no."

"I still have no idea whether it was the dishwasher or the stove that was the culprit. All I know is that my kitchen looks like London after the Blitz. And the other rooms run a close second."

"Are you all right?"

"Just a bit gritty. I was in the bedroom when the fire hit. Nobody was hurt, but my poor kitchen certainly needs additional redecorating."

"Pack a bag and come right over. You can stay as long as you need to."

"I'm packed and on my way. If I can camp out at your place through the weekend, it would be great. On Monday I have a friend who's leaving for Bermuda and I can stay at her house for two weeks. By then, hopefully, I'll be able to get back into my own apartment."

When Kate hung up, she put up some coffee and pulled out fresh linens for the bed in her small den. Laura could take her room on Saturday, but for now this would have to do. She was finishing up her hospital corners when the downstairs buzzer rang.

A minute later Laura knocked on her door. Standing there with black smudges on her cheeks and overnight case in hand, she looked completely frazzled and exhausted.

"Sorry about this."

"Don't be silly," Kate assured Laura, taking the suitcase from her hand. "I've got coffee on. Have you eaten anything?"

"I had a big choice of char-broiled items back home." Laura managed a grin. "But I found the atmosphere lacking."

Kate laughed. "Will you settle for a cheese sandwich?"

"Anything that doesn't require turning on an electric appliance. I don't want to tempt fate."

Kate decided that Laura looked much better after getting the sandwich and coffee down.

"You are a lifesaver, Kate. I hope my being here won't mess up any plans for you."

"As a matter of fact, I'm going to be out of town for the weekend. So, not only aren't you interfering with anything, it's nice to have somebody watching the place while I'm gone."

"New York?"

Kate hesitated. She'd had lunch with Laura on

217

Tuesday and told her about her plans to get together with Tony for the weekend. She'd said he was due in Boston on Saturday afternoon. So it was only natural for Laura to assume that if Kate was going to be away, she and Tony had decided to meet in New York instead.

"No," Kate muttered. "I'm not going to New York." Then, not wanting to make more of it than it was already beginning to feel like, she added, "I'm going to Montreal with a friend. Do some shopping—I could use a new wool coat—have some great dinners, see a show. . . ." She sounded just like Chris . . . and just about as believable. *Oh, my God,* she thought, *what am I doing?*

"Sounds nice," Laura said lightly, although her expression registered concerned interest. You didn't pull the wool, English or otherwise, over Laura Gladstone's eyes.

"Remember that lawyer friend of mine you met at that dinner Howell and Beck had for me?"

"The tall, dark, and handsome one who looked like he was about to fall asleep from sheer boredom?"

Kate laughed. "He was a good sport. It definitely was not his kind of party."

"I guessed that. He looked more like he belonged next door at the swinging-singles' bar."

"He's been there often enough," Kate said in a small voice. "Oh, Laura, I think I'm about to make a terrible mistake. Worse, I can't even decide if it is going to matter."

"Things that bad between you and Tony?"

"I feel like a total fool on the one hand, telling you I'm about to spend a weekend in Montreal with a man who just happens to be a whiz at seduction and then confess that I'm madly, infuriatingly, frustratingly in love with Tony. What kind of a woman loves one man and risks everything to go running off to another country with a very successful stud?"

"A woman who's confused, angry, hurt, or just plain lonely and in need of warmth and affection."

"All of the above. But something tells me I am probably going about it the wrong way."

"He isn't holding a gun on you, is he?"

"I have a terrible flaw in my personality," Kate said by way of confession. "When I start something, I feel this compulsion to see it through to the end. Besides," she added with a sigh, "I've tried every excuse in the book to get out of it. Chris is a damn good lawyer. He's got an answer for everything I throw at him." She started to clean off the kitchen table. "Maybe this is what I want: to bring the crisis to a head or something. Anything."

"Well," Laura concurred, "this should do it."

Kate went off to bed, thinking she'd be happy to change places with Laura Gladstone at that moment. A bomb going off in the kitchen would be a welcome distraction from the one ticking away in her mind.

Kate and Chris landed in Montreal at nine in the morning. They headed straight for the Hyatt Regency, one of the new luxury hotels to hit the cosmopolitan city. The sleek building was striking amid the white dusting of snow covering the city.

While Chris checked them in, Kate walked over to the currency-exchange window to convert her American cash into Canadian money. She focused on the shopping spree she intended to indulge herself in. It served the purpose of keeping her mind off Chris and her continued ambivalence about being there with him.

"All set?" Chris asked as Kate fit the new bills into her wallet, methodically arranging them in order.

She was anything but set. Her nod was barely visible. Chris ignored the frown, taking Kate's arm.

"There's an indoor swimming pool one level up. Part of a whole health club. If you don't have a suit, they give you one."

"Sounds good," she said, clearing her throat. *I could use some exercise to unwind,* she thought to herself, deciding to fit in the swim before her shopping expedition. "What time is your meeting?" She wanted hers to be a solo swim.

"I'm afraid I'll have to deposit you in your suite and then head off. I've got to get over to Rue Sherbrooke by ten. Can you manage on your own until about two?"

220

It was managing *with* Chris that she was worried about. "I'll be fine."

They rode up in a glass elevator that lifted them from the lobby to the sixteenth floor, giving them a spectacular view of the atrium around which the entire hotel was built. Kate stared down as they climbed higher, her stomach a little queasy. Heights didn't thrill her. Or maybe it was drops.

Chris wasn't watching the view. He was busy watching Kate. He wanted to put his arm around her and tell her to relax, but he knew his slightest touch would have the opposite effect. She was half frozen already, and it had nothing to do with the near-zero temperature outside.

Kate forced a smile, feeling Chris's eyes on her. "Beautiful place."

"Very beautiful," he agreed, but Kate knew he wasn't referring to the hotel.

The elevator door slid open on the sixteenth floor. Chris took Kate's elbow and steered her down to the left. The suites were located at each corner of the building. Theirs was in the northwest corner, its sweeping windows of floor-to-ceiling glass offering a panoramic vista and a perfect angle for a sunset view.

There were two adjoining sitting room–bedrooms, identical in style, although one was accented in brilliant green, the other in a sunny yellow.

"Which room would you like?" Chris asked, watching Kate check out the space. Like a tiger

221

who needed to know whether she had enough room to pounce. Or flee.

"It doesn't matter." And then, wanting to make sure Chris didn't misinterpret her statement, she hastily selected the yellow room.

Chris smiled. "Do you want to check the locks? Make sure they work?"

"Go to your meeting." She grinned, relaxing a little. This was ridiculous. Chris was, after all, a friend . . . a real friend. As Laura had said the night before, he wasn't holding a gun on her. Nothing had to happen.

The two suitcases, hers and Chris's, had been placed together in the green room. Chris lifted up Kate's and carried it over to the luggage stand by her closet.

"I reserved seats for the symphony tonight. You know the saying: 'Music soothes the soul.' " He smiled.

"Good," she said, ignoring his allusion to her feeling ill-at-ease, concentrating on the latch of her case.

"Kate." He placed his hand over the suitcase.

She looked up at him. "Chris, I tried to tell you this was a mistake. I don't know what I'm doing here."

He turned her to face him. "You're here to have a nice, fun weekend in a great city with a . . . a fairly okay guy. Last I heard, it wasn't a crime."

Kate's hint of a smile instantly vanished. She turned away. Chris cursed silently.

Had it been a crime for her to feel sorry for an innocent man locked up in prison? Was it a crime to fall in love with him . . . to want him to stop running . . . to want him to be a part of her life, not just an occasional drop-in guest?

"I'll see you at two. We can do some sight-seeing and then I'll take you to my favorite restaurant in Montreal. They've got the best dover sole this side of the English Channel." He talked fast, trying to distract her from her thoughts—thoughts that were rapidly lousing up all of his plans. It worked a little: Kate heard enough of what he was saying to nod agreement.

"See you later," he said, heading out the door.

"Have a nice meeting," she said tonelessly.

He looked back over his shoulder. She was hanging up a dress. He shrugged, turned, and left. "The best laid schemes . . ."

Kate stopped unpacking when she heard the front door close. She sat down on the bed, trying to make some sense out of the turmoil she was experiencing. She had the impulse to call Tony up, tell him she had made a complete mess of things, and ask him to . . . to what? Pack his bags and move back to Boston? Back into her life? Sure, that was what she wanted. Was it a crime?

The swimming pool was pleasantly warm, allowing Kate to do a leisurely ten laps across the pool without getting chilled. Afterward she relaxed in the whirlpool spa, ignoring the two teenagers roughhousing in the water, clearly interested in gaining her attention.

The lifeguard was also interested in getting Kate to notice him. He went about it more solicitously, bringing her a new towel when she stepped out of the spa, offering her a soda, which she turned down, and, as a last-ditch effort, asking her if she'd like to meet him after work. She could use a chaperone tonight, but she doubted this attractive Canadian had that role in mind. She smiled, explaining politely that she had other plans for the evening.

She took a few more laps under the lifeguard's disappointed eye, then headed for the shower. After she was dressed, she had a light lunch in the hotel's lobby cafe and then descended into the labyrinth of underground shops.

A whole world existed below Montreal's streets. The bitter-cold winters had led to the steady development of shopping arcades underground, allowing residents and visitors to purchase everything from croissants to designer dresses and home furnishings without ever going out of doors.

Kate wandered in and out of shops, enjoying the bargains and the charming saleswomen with their lilting French accents. At the Place Ville Marie shopping complex she found the perfect black cashmere coat, very sophisticated and very expensive. The purchase buoyed her spirits despite depleting most of her funds.

She returned to the hotel at two-fifteen to find Chris chilling a bottle of white wine.

"You look better," he said as she whirled into the room with a half a dozen boxes.

"Typical female." She laughed. "Set me loose in a store and I buy everything in sight. I charged at least a third, so I don't have to get depressed until next month, when the bills start rolling in."

She modeled the coat for Chris, who was duly complimentary. It came easy. She looked terrific. He made a mental note to send her off shopping before every planned seduction. While he poured the wine, setting hers down on the table, Kate showed him the rest of her purchases. Then she sank down on the couch and yawned.

"I think I took one lap too many in that pool. Or one shop too many. I'm wiped out."

Chris sat down beside her, handing her the wine. "Relax," he murmured softly, "we don't have to be at the restaurant until seven."

Kate took a sip of wine, the tension returning as Chris slipped his arm around her. She set the glass back down.

"I think I'll go lie down in my room for a while. A nice long nap and I'll be ready for dover sole and a soothing symphony." Her voice was firm, leaving little room for discussion.

"What time shall I awaken you?" Chris asked lamely as he watched her retreat.

"Give me two loud knocks at six." The door closed . . . and locked.

Chris finished Kate's wine, then poured himself another glass. The day was hardly going according to plan. Then again, there was still the night. He drank the glass of wine, then went downstairs.

Edgy and bored, Chris plunked himself down at the elegant bar off the lobby. He scanned the room, spotted a couple of very attractive women sitting together a few stools down, a striking brunette drinking alone at a table for two, and four businessmen haggling over a deal in a corner.

The two women at the bar paused in their talk to take note of the attractive dark-haired man ordering a Scotch on the rocks. Chris met their glance and smiled. They smiled back. The one closest to him, a honey-colored blonde, bore a slight resemblance to Kate. . . .

Another time, another place, he thought, turning away to nurse his Scotch. Maybe Kate was right. Maybe it was the challenge. She certainly made it tough enough. His usual self-confidence had a way of deserting him around Kate.

Two Scotches and several walks around the lobby later, he gave Kate's door two overly loud knocks. Immediately she answered by calling thanks, leaving Chris with the impression that she'd either been up for a while or not slept at all. He listened to the shower running next door for a few minutes, found his emerging fantasies too frustrating, and stepped into his own shower, turning the nozzle to cold for one chilling minute.

Kate knocked softly.

"I don't have the door locked," he said pointedly.

Kate walked in to find Chris sipping the remainder of the afternoon's wine, dressed in well-cut gray trousers and nothing else. "Oh, you're not ready."

Chris walked over to her. Slipping his hands around her slender waist, he murmured, "You look beautiful." His hands slid lower, his bare chest pressing lightly against the fine, thin silk of her dress.

Kate caught hold of his hands, aware of the sharp scent of liquor mingled with peppermint toothpaste on his breath. She stepped back, but Chris moved with her, ignoring the pressure of her hands on his as she tried to disentangle herself from his grasp.

She wasn't immune. There was a potent sexuality about Chris, despite the alcohol and the slightly lopsided smile. His present half-naked state made Kate uncomfortably aroused. It was a purely physical response, her mind in an altogether different place.

"You'd better finish getting dressed," she said stiffly.

Not before he bent low, kissing her seductively on the tender curve of her throat. Kate's push was more forceful than her words. Chris backed off, grinning. "That's what you get for leaving me to my fantasies all day. And for looking so delectable."

"I have a feeling most of those fantasies took place over a bottle of Scotch. And wine," she added, seeing the now empty bottle on the side table beside Chris's bed. She walked over to his closet and pulled out a shirt. "I'd better get some food into you before you get sick."

"I am not drunk," he said indignantly, saying each word very slowly to prevent himself from slurring.

Kate grinned. "You stopped at the pinky, right?"

"Right." He grinned back, taking the shirt from her hand. Instead of putting it on, he reached for her again.

"Which pinky? The fifth or the tenth?" She couldn't decide if she was alarmed by his consumption of booze or relieved. Off balance, he would be easier to cope with. Or so she thought.

Les Filles du Roy was a charming Quebecois restaurant in Vieux Montréal, the historic old section of the city. All of the waitresses were dressed in costumes typical of eighteenth-century handmaidens of the king: saucy white hats; white blouses with scooped necks and starched, puffed sleeves; and tight-bodiced aprons over simple long black skirts. The building itself was ancient but had been beautifully restored.

Kate had insisted they walk a few blocks to the restaurant, hoping the cold night air would help clear Chris's head. It worked. When the hostess led them to the greenhouse bar at the rear of the restaurant, Chris appeared reasonably sober. He ordered two glasses of wine while Kate cast an appreciative eye around the room. It had to be one of the loveliest spots she'd ever come upon.

The dover sole was as wonderful as Chris had promised. The delicious food did them both good, and although Chris finished off another bottle of wine, it was with Kate's assistance. By the time they finished up a shared dessert—a Quebecois speciality that consisted of thick slices of French bread covered with shavings of Canadian maple candy and drowned in the freshest heavy cream— their comfortable relationship had been restored.

They arrived with only five minutes to spare at the Place des Arts for the Montréal Symphony Orchestra's performance of Rimski-Korsakov's *Scheherazade.* Still giggling over a joke Chris had told on the cab ride over, Kate slid past a long row of people to her seat. Chris smiled, apologizing to everyone for disturbing them as he followed after Kate.

They settled back in their seats for the concert, Kate deciding that it was turning out to be a pleasant, enjoyable weekend after all. She put the rest of the evening out of her mind as she concentrated on the symphony's first-class rendition of *Scheherazade,* a particular favorite of hers.

After the concert Chris was all for returning straight to their suite at the hotel. Kate felt the edginess starting to resurface. She suggested a nightcap and a dance or two at the top of the Hyatt, a rooftop lounge perched over the city. Chris shrugged his consent, clearly disappointed but not wanting to refuse her anything.

It was a mistake; Kate realized that after fifteen minutes and two glasses of Scotch had disappeared down Chris's throat. After their first dance, during which she struggled to hold on to some breathing space, she decided that was as bad as watching him down those drinks.

"Let's get some sleep," she said wearily as they headed off the tiny dance floor.

"Just what I was thinking." Chris's lopsided smile had returned, along with his wandering hands. Kate gave him a dirty look and moved away as they waited for the elevator.

As they rode down, Kate stole a glance at Chris. He had that now-or-never look in his eye. The whole fragile pretense of this being a simple, unpressured weekend with a friend crumbled on the spot. It was her own fault. She knew it. She felt guilty. She realized this was about to be the end of a beautiful friendship.

Chris decided to make his move before they made it to the suite. Before Kate could safely ensconce herself behind a locked door.

"Chris, please . . ."

They were at the door to the suite. He was grabbing for her, his arms moving around her like a steel trap.

"I want you, Kate. God, how I want you. Give

230

me a chance, baby. Please?" He kissed her, trying to be tender but then becoming more demanding as she struggled to get away.

Kate pleaded with him to stop as he held on to her with one hand, unlocking the door with the other.

Chris wasn't listening. He was enflamed with a desire that shut out everything else. The intensity of his feelings clouded his mind to reason. He made himself believe she wanted him as much as he wanted her.

His hand snaked out for her breast. Kate smacked him. Not a tame, ladylike slap—a jaw-shaking, teeth-rattling swipe that sent Chris flat on his butt.

"I'm sorry if I hurt you, Chris," Kate said in much the manner of a mother scolding an exceedingly naughty boy, "but you had it coming. Maybe I had it coming too. It was a dumb idea all around. I'm in love with Tony. A fling in Montreal with a dear friend is not going to do anything but make us both miserable. And I'm still going to be in love with him." She kept moving toward her door as she spoke, relieved to reach the brass knob. "Now, I don't know about you, but I'm going to sleep and try to put this whole thing out of my mind. If I wasn't so damn mad at myself, I would be pretty angry at you. And you told me there'd be no pressure . . . you only wanted a foot in the door!" She stomped into her room.

Chris sat, dazed, petulant, the last drink repeating on him as Kate made her slow exit. Instead of a nice, warm body to make love to, he was ending up with a sound tongue-lashing, a queasy stomach, and a very sore jaw.

She locked her door, leaving Chris staring unfocused into space. As she got undressed she realized that the weekend had not been a total bust after all. It had confirmed her commitment to a man she now realized she did not—would not—spend her life without, even if it meant pulling up stakes and hiding out with him in New York.

At four in the morning there was a light rapping on her door. Kate was in a half sleep, but she woke up abruptly and fully at the sound. Her eyes focused on her packed suitcase. She was planning a quick getaway in the morning, leaving Chris to shake his hangover on his own and hopefully come to his senses.

"Kate. Are you awake?"

He sounded like his old self mixed with a touch of contriteness.

"Kate. Listen. I'm sorry. You were right. It was a dumb idea. I know you love Tony. I tried to drink myself half to death to obliterate that reality. Do you know what I think? I think we'll both be better off if you go get your man and settle down. That would resolve everything, don't you agree?"

Kate smiled to herself. "I agree."

"Yeah . . . well . . ."

"Chris."

"Hmmm."

"You still want to be friends?"

"Ummm."

"Wish me luck?"

"Don't push it, Kate." Silence. Then a couple of soft chuckles. "Yeah. I wish you luck, Kate."

"Thanks, pal."

CHAPTER THIRTEEN

Sheila Fielding was setting out the fine crystal goblets when Pete walked into the house.

"Sheila?"

"In here."

Pete walked into the dining room, loosening his tie. "Hey, what's this? Did you invite the queen for dinner tonight?"

Sheila looked up over her shoulder. "Knot your tie again, hon."

Pete groaned. "Sheila, I'm wiped out. Tony and I—"

"Where is he?"

"Tony?"

"No, the king." She grinned. "Didn't he come home with you?"

"He stayed to finish up with Barker. What gives?"

"Just a casual little dinner party."

"How come this is the first I've heard about it? And who's coming?" He leaned against the wall, arms crossed in front of him.

Sheila left off setting the table and walked over

to her husband. Putting her arms around him, she gave him one of her "Now, don't blow your stack" looks.

"Sheila . . ."

"Honey, listen. I only invited Claire Hawkins . . ."

"Who's Claire Hawkins?"

Sheila sighed, shaking her head. "I always said you never pay any attention when I talk to you."

"I'm paying attention now." He smiled, his hands moving to Sheila's waist.

"Claire's the woman I work with at Bonwit's whom I've talked about at least a hundred times."

Pete's eyebrows arched.

"All right, maybe five or six times. She's the buyer for designer sportswear. Very sharp, great taste, nice-looking . . ."

"Single?"

"Like I said, where's that brother-in-law of mine?"

"Sheila, I wish you would have let me in on your little matchmaking scheme," he muttered. "Jeez, Tony is going to—"

"He's going to have a good time for once," she said firmly. "Claire's a terrific girl."

"He's already got a terrific girl."

"Where's he keeping her, under the bed?"

"Forgive me for sounding corny"—he laughed —"but he's keeping her in his heart. And believe me, hon, there's no room left for Claire or anyone else."

Pete started to explain about Kate, stopping short when he heard the front door open. "That's just great. I was hoping Tony'd decided to take Barker out for dinner. That would have solved this whole thing."

Sheila, guilty of the same crime she'd just accused Pete of—not paying attention—busily resumed setting the table. She was certain Tony and Claire would hit it off. If he was as crazy about this other woman as Pete thought, why wasn't he with her now.

Tony, hearing voices, wandered into the dining room. He was beat, having been hard at work since seven that morning. The flu was hanging on, but he was doing his best to ignore it. All he wanted to do was get a good night's sleep and catch an early shuttle for Boston in the morning. Once he had Kate in his arms again, he knew he'd start feeling a lot better.

When he saw the table decked out and counted the four place settings, he said a silent prayer that one of them wasn't set for him. But from the smile on Sheila's face and the grimace on Pete's, he had a feeling his prayers were not about to be answered.

"You're just in time," Sheila greeted him, her smile broadening.

"For what?" he asked nervously.

"For dinner." She gave him an appraising look. "I think you can get in a quick shower, and if you want to change into something, uh, fresh . . ."

Tony threw a questioning glance at Pete, not at all happy with his brother's hasty retreat into the kitchen. "This was Sheila's idea, not mine," he called back. "Let her tell you about the party."

"Party?"

Sheila smirked. "Don't pay any attention to him. It's no big deal. I just invited a very good friend of mine over for dinner. Pete always gets uptight whenever I take the crystal out. He drinks out of paper cups so much, he thinks real glass means a formal banquet. Unless I invite somebody over, I never get the chance to use this stuff." She gave the table—set with her sterling silver, embossed china, and matching cut-crystal wine- and water glasses—a sweeping gesture. "I hope a little bit of class isn't going to intimidate you like it does your brother."

Tony wasn't biting. "Come on, Sheila. What's this all about? Who's this friend?"

"Another one with the third degree," she quipped, then caught her breath. Bad choice of words. Why was she always saying things that would remind Tony of the past. Especially now.

"Stop looking like you just got me sentenced again," he said gently. "You remind me of those people who are always struggling not to say 'Do you see what I mean?' when they're talking to a blind person."

Sheila smiled. "You're right. I've become more sensitive than you."

Tony caught her by the elbow as she started for

the kitchen. "You still haven't told me who's the fourth for dinner."

"Her name is Claire Hawkins. She's a lovely woman who works with me at Bonwit's."

"A lovely woman, huh?"

"You are as bad as your brother. She's a friend of mine. I thought it would be nice to have her for dinner. You'll like her. She's bright, pretty . . ."

"Sheila . . ."

"Don't start with me, Tony. It's one meal, for God's sake. You sit, you talk, you eat. You never have to see her again if you don't want to. I'm not keeping a shotgun in the closet. Nothing has to happen."

"Sheila, nothing is going to happen."

"Fine," she snapped. "Now, go take your shower." She started for the kitchen. "Oh, and why don't you wear that dark blue shirt? You look terrific in blue." She gave him a quick grin and disappeared behind the swinging door.

Tony laughed, then gave a low groan. This was not what he'd had in mind for tonight . . . or any night.

As he walked upstairs he could hear Pete and Sheila arguing in the kitchen. It was a little late for Pete to be filling Sheila in on the current complications of Tony's love life. One thing was for sure: He didn't need any more.

"Beautiful, Sheila." Claire Hawkins gave the dining-room table an appreciative smile. "I love Rosenthal china. Elegant yet simple."

She was holding up a plate to the light when Tony appeared, freshly showered, blue shirt on under his gray sports jacket. The scene reminded him of a commercial for dishwashing detergent he'd seen the other day on TV. He almost laughed, waiting for the tall, dark-haired woman to say "No streaks!" He cleared his throat to eliminate the urge.

Sheila and Claire looked up at the same moment, each giving Tony a private appraisal. Sheila was pleased. He looked less haggard, and the shirt was perfect. Claire was pleasantly surprised. Most blind dates fell far short of their marks. Not that she'd had many. But finding attractive, single men in New York City wasn't easy when you were almost thirty and had to compete with thousands of love-starved twenty-two-year-olds.

Sheila made the introductions. Claire stifled a nervous flutter as he greeted her. Tony hoped he displayed the proper amount of polite interest. He had to admit that Claire Hawkins was better-looking than he had expected. It had been a long time since he'd had to suffer through awkward blind dates. Maybe tonight wouldn't be so awful. As Sheila had said, nothing had to happen.

"Can I get you two a drink?" Sheila asked, trying to relax. Between Pete's harangue and Tony's lack of enthusiasm, she was beginning to feel like a wreck. Pete was probably right—not that she was about to admit it to him at this point. She should have left well enough alone.

"Do you have Dubonnet?" Claire asked.

Sheila shook her head. Claire would have to pick the one drink she didn't have. "How about wine? Or Scotch, vodka, gin . . . a beer?" No, Claire was definitely not a beer drinker.

"A beer would be great," Tony piped in.

Perfect, Sheila thought.

Claire chose wine. "White, if you have it?"

"White? Oh, sure. Chablis or . . ." She went to check the label. ". . . Riesling?"

"The Riesling. It's a nice, fruity wine." Turning to Tony, she said, "I've gone to a few wine tastings over the past couple of years. Ever since my vacation to France. I went on this marvelous tour of the wine regions."

Tony smiled. The last he had heard, Dubonnet was not one of the finer French wines.

He poured his beer into a mug. "It must have been fun."

"Terrific."

"Well, I'd better see to the roast . . . and to Pete. He's usually the first one down to the dinner table," Sheila said.

Tony could have told her Pete was taking his sweet time upstairs to avoid this little scene, but he was sure she already knew that.

"Want me to see what's happening with Pete?"

"No, no. You two relax. Get acquainted. I'll be back in a few minutes."

They studied their drinks solemnly, taking careful sips. Tony looked across at Claire at precisely the same moment she looked across at him.

Smiles. Was that a hint of seductiveness he detected in hers? He finished off his beer.

"So . . . how do you and Sheila know each other?"

"Through work. I'm at Bonwit's. Actually, I do all their East Coast sportswear purchasing. It's a really good job. I started out in sales, but this was what I was working toward. Not that I want to stop with sportswear," she assured him: the ideal, self-directed career woman. "I plan to make it into designer fashions one of these days. That would move me into a whole other world. I'd get to travel abroad, something I absolutely adore. Probably because I spent my whole childhood in a little town in Iowa no larger than this neighborhood."

Tony nodded, gave Claire an understanding smile, and hoped she'd continue to do all the talking for the evening. It let him off the hook.

"What about you? Sheila tells me you're really doing marv— great in real estate."

"I'm coming along."

"Don't be modest," she said coyly, observing him critically. "I bet you're the kind of man who's successful at anything he tries."

Tony had to laugh. "Not everything. Believe me."

"Well . . . I don't. But it's nice to meet a man who doesn't go around tooting his own horn all the time."

"Can I get you some more wine?"

Another coy smile. "I'd better not," she said. "I tend to talk a lot when I've had one too many. When I was in France that summer, drinking all that wine, let me tell you, I bent a few ears. Most people didn't know what I was talking about. They didn't understand more than five words of English, and the only thing I could say in French was *merci.*" She laughed, pleased to see Tony's smile. For a minute there she thought she might be talking too much now.

For the next ten minutes, with Pete still hiding upstairs and Sheila banging pots in the kitchen, Tony fed Claire one or two questions and sat back, letting her "bend his ear." Fortunately one glass of wine was doing the trick this evening. He had the feeling that, cold sober, Claire could talk most people round the flagpole. Which suited him just fine. Except for the fact that Claire was overly eager to please, the evening was proving to be tolerable.

Pete walked into the living room, shook hands with Claire, gave Tony a bleak smile, and hastily excused himself to go help Sheila with the dinner.

The interruption in Claire's flow of chatter brought her up short. Oh, God, she was running off at the mouth again. She couldn't even remember what she'd been saying when Pete zoomed in and then out of the room. She guessed that if she asked Tony to cue her, he wouldn't be able to. What was the matter with her? She was trying too hard, that was what. *Slow down, Claire,* she thought. *Take a deep breath and ask the questions. Give Tony a chance to get a word in edgewise.*

It was the wrong tack. If Tony was quiet and mildly disinterested in her prattle before, he grew tense and uneasy now as she began asking him about himself. She was relieved when Sheila called them in for dinner. So was Tony.

Sheila carried the ball through the meal. She was determined to get her uncomfortable audience to relax. By dessert she had accomplished her goal. She got Tony and Pete to share some amusing stories about work; she told three of the latest jokes she'd heard in the men's department where she worked; and Claire did a terrifically funny imitation of the typical Bonwit shopper looking for "something amusing to wear to Palm Springs."

They drank coffee in the living room. Pete, deciding this evening wasn't turning into the disaster he feared, began to act like his old self. He was just getting going with his amusing anecdotes about the adventures he and Tony had as young boys, when Sheila interrupted him mid-sentence.

"I almost forgot, Pete. We promised the Fogels we'd drop off those slides of Florida tonight. You two don't mind, do you? It completely slipped my mind. They're our neighbors down the block. They're going to Florida next week, and I promised them . . ." She stopped, flushing. "We won't be long. Not too long."

"I think they get your message, Sheila." Pete laughed.

Tony wasn't laughing. It was one thing to spend the evening as a foursome, but he had no desire to be left alone with Claire for the next couple of hours. He had to catch an early flight to Boston the next day.

When Sheila ushered Pete out, Claire looked over at Tony. "Not too subtle, was she?"

Tony laughed. "Only if you call a ton of bricks subtle." He fought back a yawn.

Claire decided to ignore the message that Tony was tired and would probably like nothing better than to take her home and say good-bye. It was Saturday night; she hadn't been out on a date in months with a man she felt had possibilities. Tony Fielding had possibilities. It was up to her to prove to him that she did too.

She poured more coffee into his cup and sat down beside him. "Marvelous dinner."

He had a faint smile on his lips. "Marvelous."

She felt like kicking herself. Concentrating on a loose thread at the cuff of her blouse, she said, "Pete mentioned you used to live in Boston. I have a brother there. He lives in the Back Bay. Teaches at Boston University. I love visiting him." She forgot the thread. "I think Boston is a very exciting city. It's big enough to have all the cultural advantages and small enough to retain a sense of charm.

Actually, I've often thought of moving there. Bonwit's has a branch two blocks from my brother's apartment." She grinned. "There I go, doing all the talking again. So, how come you left Boston? Were you in real estate there?"

"No."

Claire looked at him quizzically.

"I used to be an investment counselor." He forced a laugh. "Past history."

Claire knew she had touched on something troubling, but for the life of her she couldn't figure out what. Maybe he had been a flop at something. How awkward if he'd been fired and had to go work for his brother in order to make a buck.

"Well, real estate sounds more exciting to me. I bet it must be very rewarding. Your brother seems thrilled to have you here."

"Claire . . ."

"Yes." She prepared herself for rejection. After years of dating, she could tell when it was coming.

"I just got out of prison six months ago. I have a feeling Sheila, out of concern for me—and you—conveniently forgot to mention it."

Whatever she was expecting, it wasn't that. She stared at him, open-mouthed, then quickly pursed her lips. She was, for once, completely at a loss for words.

"I was found guilty of embezzling funds from the investment company I worked for."

"Oh," she swallowed hard. How come she had the lousiest luck when it came to men? Here she'd thought she had found herself a real winner, and he turns out to be an ex-con—an ex-con she was sitting alone with in the house of a woman she knew only in the most casual of terms.

"I'm harmless." He smiled, understanding some of the thoughts careening through her mind.

She forced a smile. "It's . . . it's a surprise." She flushed. "I mean . . . I wasn't expecting that."

Tony felt compassion for the flustered woman sitting beside him. "I don't suppose, when a friend fixes you up on a blind date, you expect the guy to have just spent the last year in the clink."

"No."

Why was he doing this? he wondered. Here was a woman who hadn't the slightest knowledge about his past. It would have been so easy to slip right over those fourteen months. Wasn't this why he was here in New York—to relate to people without those concrete walls creeping up on him again? Was he finally coming to grips with reality, or simply looking for an effective way to give Claire Hawkins the brush-off?

"I'm trying to bury the past. Start fresh. It isn't easy."

"I . . . I guess it isn't." She focused on that thread on her blouse again, anxiously listening for the return of Sheila and Pete.

"Claire, you can relax. I . . . I just thought you ought to know."

There was something so gentle and sympathetic

in his tone, she found herself smiling. "I've never known anybody who's been in prison before. I guess I . . . felt a little panicky." She flushed. "Embezzlement isn't like . . ." The words wouldn't come.

"Like murder or rape. No, it's not like that," he said tonelessly. "White-collar crime, they call it."

"Yes, I know," she said, her smile sympathetic. He liked her better now than he had all evening.

"I was eventually acquitted. They found out my cries of innocence were legit after a very special friend of mine discovered the real criminal. I'd be on parole now . . . if it wasn't for her."

In one brief speech Claire had her hopes buoyed, then shattered. So he did have potential . . . and a girl friend.

"I have to catch an early flight for Boston in the morning. Can I take you home?"

Claire stood up. "No. That's all right. I drove over in my car. I only live a few miles from here. South Yonkers. It's not a bad spot. I . . ." *Shut up and go home, Claire,* she told herself.

Tony walked into the hallway with her and helped her on with her coat.

"It was very nice meeting you," he said so formally that he laughed. Claire laughed too. "I mean it," he said, this time the words ringing true. "Most evenings when I come back from a long day at the coal mines, I grab a quick bite and head up to my room to do some work or read. This was far more pleasant."

247

"Thanks. I had a nice time too. Got thrown for a couple of minutes, but . . ."

"You pulled through marvelously."

They laughed again. "I promise never to use that word again if we ever do have another evening together."

He smiled. A good-bye smile. A smile that said "You're a nice lady, Claire, but I have other plans." She smiled back. Oh, well, it was an interesting night anyway.

After Claire left, Tony took an ice-cold beer from the fridge and went into the den to call Kate.

He was surprised to hear another woman's voice say hello. It was a voice he vaguely recognized.

"Is Kate Stuart in?"

"Tony?"

"Yes. Who am I talking to?"

"Laura. Laura Gladstone. How are you, stranger? Gee, all it took was for my house to catch fire to get to say hello to you again."

"Laura, what's going on?"

"I'm Kate's surprise houseguest for the weekend. My apartment is . . . Let's just say it's getting a much-needed face lift."

"Can I talk to Kate?"

"Afraid she isn't here."

Was that a note of uneasiness in her voice?

"Where is she?"

"She's . . . out of town. Montreal."

"Montreal? I just spoke to her yesterday. She

248

didn't mention anything about being out of town. Laura, is something the matter? Is Kate all right?"

"Tony, she's fine. Honest. I don't really know the details. I showed up as she was leaving."

"Why don't I believe you're telling me everything you know, Laura?"

"She should be home early tomorrow. She did mention she had a lot of work to catch up on before Monday," she said, trying to appease him. "Why don't you call then and find out the details from her?"

"I will do better than that: I'll be there waiting for her when she gets home. See you in the morning, Laura. Oh, and by the way, you may be great in Personnel, my friend, but you're a lousy liar."

"What do you want? I never did strive for success in that field."

After hanging up with Laura, Tony rang up Chris on impulse. He'd feel less uneasy upon hearing his voice.

The answering service informed him that Chris Coleman was in Montreal for the weekend on business. He was due back early Sunday afternoon.

Tony had a damn good idea just what that business was. Chris had warned him, hadn't he?

How could Kate do it? Tony wondered. *One day she's near to tears because I can't get up to see her for the weekend, and the next day she's having herself a grand old time in Montreal with a guy who she's always professing is just a good friend.* He stared down at his tightfisted grip on the telephone, his anger escalating by the second. And along with the anger, despair. He wouldn't just open the door and let another woman stroll out of his life. Not this time. Not this woman.

He grabbed his coat and stormed out the door, bumping into Sheila and Pete on their way in. Sheila gave a quick look over Tony's shoulder for Claire.

"Did she go home?"

"Who?" Tony snapped, Claire having completely disappeared from his mind.

"Claire," Sheila answered, incredulous. What was the matter with him?

Pete didn't know what was the matter, but he recognized the signals of a storm about to hit. Ushering a confused Sheila inside the house, he told her he was going to take a walk with Tony.

"Walk? It's below freezing out there," she muttered as he closed the front door.

For two blocks the brothers walked in silence. When Pete thought Tony had burned off enough steam to talk, he said, "Kate, right?"

"Yeah."

Another half a block. Tony stopped short. "She's having an affair with . . . a friend of mine."

Pete flapped his arms against his chest to keep his teeth from chattering. This wasn't the greatest night for walking.

"Are you sure?"

Tony cast him a grim smile.

250

"She told you?"

"She's away. In Montreal. With the guy."

"That's it? Those are all the details you've got?"

"Come on, Pete. You haven't been married that long. Have you forgotten what a man and woman do when they go off together for a weekend?"

"Slow down, Tony. I've been on a few weekends in my day. And since it's all water under the bridge, now that I don't have any reputation to maintain, a few of those weekends were a flop. You don't always score, pal. At least I didn't. Maybe you had better luck."

Pete's point slowly registered in Tony's brain. "Kate isn't the type of woman who . . . who leads a guy on. At least, she didn't with me."

"Maybe you're special. Just like she is."

Tony studied his brother carefully. "She is special. I don't want to lose her."

"Then why are we standing out here in subzero temperature? Go pack an overnight bag and find out what that trip was all about."

The sun was barely rising over Montreal as Kate boarded her plane. Chris had been tactful enough to remain asleep, letting her get away without a hitch. All she wanted to do now was arrive in New York and throw herself in Tony's arms. Landing time was eight-fifteen A.M.

The shuttle to Boston arrived on the hour. Tony checked his watch. Seven-fifty. Ten more minutes and he'd be landing at Logan Airport. Another twenty to Kate's apartment. He would be there when she walked in . . . and he'd be waiting for an explanation. He hoped with all his heart that she had a good one.

CHAPTER FOURTEEN

The taxi pulled up in front of a brown-trimmed white house. Kate checked the number on the door. Yes, this was the one. She smoothed her hair distractedly, then fished in her purse for the cab fare.

Walking up the narrow slate path, Kate felt a little foolish arriving on the doorstep, overnight case in hand. Lady on the lam. She smiled to herself as she rang the doorbell.

No answer. Where was her head? It was Sunday morning, not even nine A.M. Everybody still was probably asleep. Great way to meet Tony's brother and sister-in-law for the first time, waking them up at nearly the crack of dawn.

As she stood at the door, deciding whether to ring again or go get a cup of coffee and call from the restaurant, she heard a shuffling sound, then the release of the lock.

The two women stood facing each other, Kate, nervous, embarrassed; Sheila, puzzled, irritated at being awakened on her one morning off.

"Yes?" Sheila's voice, usually low-pitched, was hoarse now.

"I'm Kate Stuart . . . a friend of Tony's," she said. She should have called. Of course, she should have called. "I'm sorry to awaken you."

The light was beginning to seep through Sheila's cloudy head. "Tony's friend? From Boston?" Sheila pulled her terry robe closer to her chest, the blast of cold air finally piercing her grogginess.

"Yes." Well, at least Tony'd said something.

"Where's my head?" Sheila chuckled. "Still in bed, probably. Come on in before we both freeze to death."

Kate stepped inside, apologizing again. She saw Sheila's eyes rest for a moment on her suitcase.

"I flew in directly from Montreal. I . . . I came early because I didn't want to miss Tony. I know he had to work today."

Just as Sheila was about to explain that Tony wasn't there, Pete appeared at the bottom of the staircase.

"Who's there, Sheila?"

"Come on into the living room and meet a friend of Tony's."

"One minute."

Kate could hear him climbing back up the stairs.

"He's gone to make himself decent." Sheila grinned. "I need some coffee. How about you?"

Kate nodded. "Sounds great." She followed Sheila into the kitchen. "Tony must be wiped out from that flu. I'll have that cup of coffee and then I'll take off for a while and let him sleep."

"He's not sleeping. I heard him leave very early this morning."

"For Boston." Pete grinned, shaking his head as he stood at the entry to the kitchen. "This, I believe, is what is known as a comedy of errors. He's probably at your apartment at this very moment." He walked closer, smiling at Kate. "It's nice to meet you—finally. Tony's got very good taste."

Kate smiled. "Thanks. But what do you mean, he's in Boston? He called me Friday to say he couldn't—"

"He also called you last night and learned that you were in Montreal."

"I still don't follow."

"He's in Boston, ready for a showdown, Kate." He looked embarrassed and uncomfortable. "He thinks your weekend in Montreal may have been . . ." He tried another approach. "He knows you didn't go up there alone."

"Oh." It was Kate's turn to feel embarrassed. She looked from Pete to Sheila, then back to Pete again. Sheila handed her a cup of coffee. Kate stared down at the black brew. "What a mess. What a complete mess."

Pete patted her shoulder. "Tony's crazy about you, Kate. In case you didn't know that."

"I do know it. *I* love *him* too. But we certainly do get our signals crossed." She gave him a wry smile. "Especially at this moment."

Pete grinned. Sheila was slow at putting the pieces together. She poured coffee for herself and Pete. They sat together around the kitchen table.

"Could I use your phone? I'd better call him, or else he's likely to take off for New York just when I land in Boston."

"He'll wait around for a while. Why not give him some time to cool down? Sheila, how about some breakfast?"

Kate interrupted. "No, really. I couldn't . . . I've ruined your morning already."

"Hey, come on. I've been as curious as hell to get to meet this woman Tony's fallen head over heels in love with," Pete assured her.

"I've wanted to meet you two as well," Kate said. "Tony's told me so much about you, especially about how you helped him through those long, awful months in jail."

"I should have gone up to see him more often," Pete said, shaking his head. "God, that place was a nightmare. It nearly killed me seeing him there."

"I know," Kate said softly. "Tony understood how you felt. It was your caring and love that mattered to him."

Sheila sighed. "I wish there was some way to help him push past that awful time. He's still not himself. But he puts up a good front, right, Pete?"

"He's talking a little more. I keep encouraging him. At first I thought that if he wanted to keep silent about his experience, I should respect that. After hearing him wake up screaming in the mid dle of the night a few times, I realized holding everything inside wasn't going to do him an ounce of good. He sees that too. It's just, well, I can understand only so much. Some of that hell he went through can't be shared. He tries damn hard not to stay bitter about it, but I can't honestly blame him if the rage still gets the better of him on occasion."

Kate nodded. "And his hurt. I kept wishing it would disappear. I wanted him to feel whole, free." Her voice caught. "I've been very selfish, telling myself it would be better for Tony to come back to Boston than for me to come here with him. I've lived in Boston for ten years, and in the same apartment for seven. I have a terrific job, great advancement opportunities, lots of friends. It's . . it's home."

"Kate, I'll be honest with you," Pete said. "I adore having Tony here. I love him and he happens to be a terrific real estate broker. But I'm selfish too. I still feel like the big brother looking out for my kid brother, who's been through hell. I want to protect him. I want to take the bitterness and hurt away. I want to pretend being here is the best thing for him. But you know something? You are right. He probably would be able to make more progress in Boston. He still feels ashamed of what happened to him. He hates socializing because he's afraid the topic will come up. He doesn't want to have to explain every time, but he can't bear the thought of people thinking he's some kind of a criminal. He's got himself between a rock and a hard place. And as much as I want to, I can't push him free."

Sheila, listening as she made some toast and scrambled eggs, joined them again at the table. "I think all of us want so much to help him that none of us is accepting him where he's at. Maybe we have to give him more time. How long would it take any of us to cope with that kind of an experience?"

"That's a good question," Kate said. "That's why I'm here. I finally realized that if I love Tony I have to do exactly what you just said: take him where he's at. I was expecting to be telling that to him face-to-face. If Tony still wants me to, I'm ready to move to New York."

"What about your job, your friends?"

Kate smiled at Pete. "There are other jobs." She shrugged. "I have to do something, Pete. I can't just let him drift out of my life. Sure, I could make a staunch stand for my independence, my career, my self-righteous beliefs about what I think is best for Tony . . . and for me. I've . . . I've done that once before. Not that it's always wrong to hold to your principles, but sometimes you can end up losing more than you gain. This is one of those times."

Pete squeezed Kate's hand. "I hope it works out."

Kate called home. Laura answered. Tony'd been there and left.

"He was in quite a state, Kate. I'd better warn

you, he's fit to be tied. Sat here for exactly twenty minutes—What am I saying, 'sat.' He paced back and forth so many times, I was beginning to get seasick. Then all of a sudden he stormed toward the door and said to forget he ever showed up. To quote him, 'It's her life.' End quote. Very short but not too sweet. What should I do if he reappears?"

"Tell him I'm sitting in Yonkers, waiting for him to come home."

Kate told Pete and Sheila the latest. She rubbed her eyes, exhaustion washing over her. She'd had very little sleep in the last couple of nights.

Sheila put her arm around Kate. "Come on, I'll show you to Tony's room and you can catch a little shut-eye. He's probably on his way back here now, and there's nothing to do but wait."

Kate tried to refuse, feeling she'd already disrupted their lives enough for one day, but Sheila, joined by Pete, refused to listen to her arguments.

"You'll be able to cope with my fiery brother better if you get some sleep," Pete assured her.

Kate had to agree. Right now she couldn't think straight. Here she was, feeling giving, loving, ready to meet Tony's demands, and he was working himself up into a rage over her supposed infidelity. It was bound to be quite a reunion. She decided to forego politeness for slumber.

Arguments spun around in Tony's head. They'd been spinning since the previous night. By the time he arrived at Kate's house that morning, he had already gone through and rejected dozens.

Now, sitting on the shuttle back to New York, he had this crazy impulse to tell the pilot to turn around and take him to Boston again. What was the use? He'd said it all to Laura. It was Kate's life.

Damn it. It was his life too. He stared blankly out the window. A sense of helplessness, like that which he had felt so often in prison, washed over him.

In the fifty-six minutes it took the shuttle to travel from Boston to New York, Tony tried to think logically, realistically, honestly. He strove to put everything into a sensible perspective, but he was nowhere nearer resolving the situation in his mind than he had been when he'd hung up on Chris Coleman's answering service the night before.

He rubbed his eyes, yawning. He was exhausted. He hadn't slept all night. Although he had tried to calm down, he had been too edgy to close his eyes. Then this morning with Laura. Again too edgy. Couldn't sit still. Couldn't wait. He needed to do something. Take action. What action? At this moment she was probably nestled in bed with Chris in some hotel room in Montreal.

The pain shot through him again. Katie, Katie. He shut his eyes tightly, the cabdriver shouting him awake as the taxi pulled up in front of Pete's house a half hour later.

Groggily, Tony pulled out some bills, paid the fare, and walked slowly up the drive, digging into his pocket for the key to the kitchen entrance. He stepped quietly into the house, remembering through his fog that it was Sunday, a cherished day of sleeping late for Pete and Sheila. Then he realized that Pete wouldn't be in bed this morning. He'd agreed to take over for Tony today so that his kid brother could go flying off half-cocked to Boston to confront the woman he'd so foolishly left behind. The accusations, the indignation, the rage, still churned inside him, unrequited, hurting.

His hand gripped the banister tightly as he climbed the stairs. Sleep. He let his mind focus on that one thought. Maybe after he had some sleep he'd be able to think more clearly, figure out his next step . . . figure out if there was a next step.

The room was dark, the shades still drawn. Hadn't he raised them when he'd awakened at dawn? He must not have. He let them be; the darkness was soothing. Leaning against the back of his desk chair, he slipped his shoes off, lifted his jersey over his head, and flung it on the desk. He stretched, the idea of sleep absorbing him fully for the moment.

He stumbled over something in the dark. Too tired to think about it or move whatever it was out of the way, he stepped around the obstacle and sank down onto the mattress.

They both screamed at the same time. Kate, awakened by the feel of a body next to her, sprang into a sitting position. Tony had already leaped up and out of the bed, in total shock.

He flicked on the light switch. Kate blinked, then quickly blocked out the glare with her hands. "Tony?"

"What the . . . ? Kate?" If, for one million bucks, he'd been asked to name the last person in the world who would be sitting up in his bed just then, he would have picked Kate and become a very rich man.

As it was, he was simply a guy stunned out of his exhaustion, mouth gaping open at the sight of Kate squinting up at him as she slowly adjusted to her own shock.

"Hi." She smiled tentatively, not sure about his mood.

He helped clarify it for her. "What are you doing here?" he asked gruffly.

"I was sleeping," she answered, her eyes studying him more closely now, as the light no longer bothered her. He looked wiped out but very sensual, provocative, standing there bare-chested, hair mussed, eyes burning into her. She was stunned by her own immediate arousal. Her fingers gripped the comforter against her blouse. She felt the urge to fling it aside, beg him to climb into the bed beside her and undress her. *Warm me,* she thought. *Hold me close. This is what I'm doing here. I'm here for you to love me.*

"I thought you would still be in Montreal." The harsh tone of anger didn't fade.

Kate sighed. No, he wasn't going to climb in beside her at this moment. Explanations. That's what he was waiting for. She gave a silent order to her body to calm down. It didn't obey.

"Tony, I—"

"What happened? Don't tell me Chris turned out to be a disappointment," he said, seething. "Or are you here to make comparisons? See which of us is better?" He took hold of her wrist as she tried to push a lock of hair from her forehead.

"Stop this, Tony. If you settle down, I'll explain."

"Oh, I bet. I bet you have some explanations. Go on, tell me. Tell me I deserved it. I left you sitting alone for the weekend, broke a date because I'm busting my chops, trying to make a life for myself again—a life for us. . . . What was it, Kate? Spite? Temptation? The realization that Chris was the wiser choice? Or just a little fling to keep you from feeling bored this weekend?"

Unconsciously his hand gripped her tighter, his other hand clasping her shoulder so that she was pinned to the bed. His knees pressed against her thighs on the mattress, his face only inches from hers.

"Please let go of me. You're hurting me."

For a minute the words didn't sink through. When they did, he dropped his hands so abruptly, he fell back onto the pillows. He stayed in his kneeling position, looking down at her. Suddenly

263

the heat of his anger switched to such a piercing feeling of passion, he moaned out loud.

Kate sat up, reaching out for him, but he turned away from her. "No, Kate. It's been a hopeless struggle all along." He looked over his shoulder at her. She met his gaze, wide-eyed and silent. "I didn't mean to hurt you," he said. A glimmer of a smile. "Maybe I did. I don't know. I haven't been able to think straight. . . . Here I'd been telling you I couldn't think straight in prison and now . . . now I don't seem much better at it." His head sank into the palms of his hands. Kate saw his chest heave, but there were no sounds. She touched his back. He allowed the touch but didn't respond, head still bowed low.

"I love you, Tony," she whispered. "Chris never stood a chance. I knew that the minute I agreed to go to Montreal with him." She stroked his back, her hands gently kneading the tight, hard muscles, feeling an ever-so-slight give. "I don't know why I went. Maybe it was partly spite, a touch of temptation, hurt, frustration. I'm far from perfect, Tony. I don't always know the right thing to do."

"Neither do I." He lifted his head, turning to face her. "That's why I left your apartment this morning. I realized I didn't know what to do about my fury, my fears, my desperate desire not to lose you. . . . At the very same time, I felt I couldn't really hold on to you."

"Hold on to me, Tony. That's what I want. I want it so badly."

"Katie . . ."

She took his hands and placed them around her waist. "See? It isn't so hard." She leaned up against him, her lips pressed to his ear. "Nothing happened in Montreal. I'm innocent. Do you believe me?"

She felt him shiver, felt his arms press her more tightly to him, giving her the answer she was waiting for. "You're the only one I want, the only one who can give me a sense of completeness," she murmured, her eyes welling with tears. "Nothing is hopeless. Remember all those times I said those words in that awful waiting room. We'd sit on that dreary blue couch and I'd tell you that something good was in the air. I could feel it." She placed her hands on his face, staring closely into his eyes. "I feel it now. Call it woman's intuition. Call it love." She smiled her sweetest smile.

It tore right at Tony's heart. "I'm so crazy about you, Katie. I'm sorry. I'm so sorry."

She shook her head, her smile fuller. "You're very sexy when you're inflamed by jealousy. It's probably not the ideal way to learn how much I mean to you, but I'll take it for now."

"You mean everything to me." He sighed, stretching out alongside her on the bed.

Tony held her for a long time. Without intending to, they fell asleep, their passion taking second place to relief and sheer exhaustion. Kate was stirred awake by a light rapping sound on wood.

Sheila's voice came through the closed door. "I'm going out. Pete and I won't be back till six. See you."

"Thanks, Sheila," Kate said, smiling.

Tony stretched. "Hi, Goldilocks."

"Hi."

Her eyes sparkled, greeting him with warmth and hunger. He took her hand, pressing it to his lips. Then teasingly he nipped a finger.

"Ouch." She laughed. Happy, carefree laughter. It had been awhile. . . .

She snuggled closer, pressing her head into the crook of his arm, stretching her other hand across his naked chest. "We have a lot to talk about," she murmured.

"Later."

She looked up at him, laughing again. "Tell me something, Papa Bear. Are we in Yonkers or in heaven?"

He touched her mouth, his finger drawing a line across her lower lip. Then he slipped his hand under her crumpled blouse, pressing his palm against her lacy bra. "Heaven."

She undid the tiny pearl buttons and he slipped the blouse off her shoulders. He helped her with the rest of her clothes, reveling in the exquisitely silky feel of her smooth, warm skin. He undressed hurriedly, hugging her tightly as he slipped under the covers beside her. This was the last thing in the world he expected today. The last . . . and yet, what he wanted most. Had wanted all along. He didn't know how to bring her back into his arms. But Katie had found the way, as she had before. His temptress, his haven, his love.

Their lips met, his tongue caressing hers, darting inside her mouth, hungry for her. She moaned softly, curving into him so that she could feel his warmth along her entire body. Their hands explored each other, relishing this treasured time, sensing that something new and important was indeed in the air. Call it intuition. Call it love.

He covered her body with greedy kisses, running his hands over her breasts, down the curves and shadows of her body. Moist, eager kisses over full, ripe breasts, softly rounded hips, firm, slender legs. His caresses impatient yet tender, his senses reeling with the feel, the scent, the taste, of her.

Her fingers gripped him, her body straining to receive each kiss, lost in a rush of passion, her pulse racing. She abandoned herself to the desire that had been building since she'd first awakened to find him in the room. Her hands lovingly moved over him, searching, stroking, exploring in ways that made him cry out in pleasure, his hot breath against her satin skin.

He rolled onto his side, taking Kate with him. She arched against him, intoxicated by the heat engulfing them. She cupped his face, kissing him, her tongue probing, tempting. He kissed her back, hard, almost hurting, the tender pain inflaming her more. She whispered his name over and over, her hands more insistent and enticing as she continued to caress him.

A throbbing sensation spread like a million fiery sparks through her body. She moved on top of him, encircling his calves with her legs, guiding him inside her, crying out with a fierce joy as he cupped her buttocks, pulling her hard against him. They moved together, their rhythm increasing to a feverish pitch. Kate clutched him as he grasped her hips, urging her faster, whispering her name, then catching his breath as the trembling, shuddering sensations took over his body.

Her breath came in quick gasps and then a long, drawn-out moan of pleasure, followed by Tony's, as they uninhibitedly shared that cherished moment of fulfillment. She collapsed against him, then started to roll off of him, but Tony held her tightly. "Don't leave me," he whispered hoarsely.

"Never." She lay on top of him, her fingers gently stroking the line from his shoulder to his wrist. He captured her hand, held it tight, brought it to his lips.

"What do we do now, Kátie?" His voice was so whisper-soft, she could barely make out his words.

"We stop this crazy commuting, for one thing," she answered, feeling his body tense. She moved off him and, propping herself up on an elbow, looked down at him. "I'm going to move here . . . well, not exactly here." She smiled. "I'd like us to get our own place so that we don't have to make your poor sister-in-law beat any more hasty retreats so we can be alone."

"Katie, you can't do that. You hate New York."

"I can learn to live with it . . . better than I can learn to live without you."

"But your job . . ."

"There are other jobs," she said with a confidence she did not altogether feel. Tony knew her too well to believe it himself.

"I can't ask you to do this, Kate. You'd be giving up too much."

"How long are we going to last this way? I want us to last forever. Don't you understand that?"

He smiled, cupping her face in his hands. "I understand." His hands dropped; his eyes closed. "You'd rather I came back to Boston, wouldn't you?"

It was an old argument, played out too many times, the ending always the same. He couldn't go back. He wanted a new life, with no familiar faces who knew him as the man who'd spent fourteen painful, agonizing months in prison for a shameful crime. The news of his acquittal had appeared on a back page of the local papers—a small blurb many people would not have noticed. So he was constantly meeting people who knew only that he was now out of prison. They still looked at him as if he were a criminal. Worse, he still felt like one at those times. Shame was a terrible thing, and in all these months Kate had not come up with a way to help him erase it.

"I want us to have a chance—a chance to be just two people together, two people in love. I want the wounds to heal, Tony. If they'll heal here, then this is where we have to be."

"I still think you'd be giving up a hell of a lot."

"Then you'll have to give me a lot to make up for it." She smiled provocatively.

"I'll give you everything I've got." He pulled her to him and they began to make love again.

It was getting close to six o'clock. They dressed hurriedly, grinning at each other in illicit pleasure. Shirt in hand, he walked over to Kate, encircling her with his arms. "I think we should get married."

"That's part of the everything I want."

They were kissing when Pete shouted up the stairs that he was home.

CHAPTER FIFTEEN

"Your résumé is very impressive, Miss Stuart."
Harris Roberts was a thickset man in his middle
fifties. He peered over the typed sheet to study the
tall, attractive blonde across from him. "To be perfectly honest, it's too impressive. The position we
have open at this time doesn't come close to the
one you are in now."

"Unfortunately, Mr. Roberts, my current job is
in Boston. I'm planning to get married and move
to New York. I realize I am unlikely to find a starting position to match my job at Howell and Beck.
I'm looking for a company I can grow with."

"Yes . . . well, the problem as I see it, Miss
Stuart, is that right now our firm is in an econo-
mizing phase. I'm sure, being an accountant, you
can understand. . . ."

She understood. After three days of job interviews, the picture was becoming crystal clear:
"You're overqualified"; "You're underqualified";
"We can't afford you." And then the far more subtle message: Women don't make it up to executive
positions very easily. No, they have to do some-

thing spectacular, Kate thought, like stop an embezzlement operation.

She smiled politely at Harris Roberts. Yes, she'd think about the salary offer. Yes, he'd certainly pursue the possibility of increasing it sometime in the near future . . . hopefully. He'd think about it. She'd think about it. Scratch one more interview.

She stopped in the ladies' room on her way out of the building. Studying her face in the mirror, she wondered what kind of makeup she could apply that would smooth out the bleak look of depression she saw. She was meeting Tony for lunch in twenty minutes. He'd be able to tell immediately the interview had been a bust. As had the others. It just wasn't easy to find a job that came near to the one she had at Howell and Beck. Kate told herself that wasn't the important thing, but looking at herself, she knew she was lying.

She applied some rouge, took out the barrettes in her hair, and combed it loose the way Tony liked. She smiled to herself in the mirror. That was better. She still had to get through an afternoon of apartment hunting. They were looking for a place that Tony could move into right away, Kate joining him when he was settled.

After she had shared her decision with Tony to move to New York, she'd returned to work and put in for a week's vacation for the following Monday. Now here she was, making the rounds. Tony had insisted she see what was available in New

York before giving Howell and Beck her notice. Kate had reluctantly agreed. Having made her decision, she'd wanted to act on it right away but Tony had seen through her eagerness to the fears beneath the surface. She was afraid, he told her, that she might back down once she saw that good jobs were tough to find and decent apartments were double the rent they were in Boston. He wanted her to face the situation squarely. She believed she'd be better off if she just jumped right in and let the chips fall where they may. A fait accompli. But Tony had been adamant.

Tony was reading through the apartment ads when Kate stole up behind him, put her arms around his chest, and gave him a moist kiss on the back of his neck. "Guess who?"

He took hold of her hands, closing his eyes. "Mmmm. Suzanne? Melissa? Barbie?"

Kate bit his earlobe. "Guess again."

He looked up, grinning. "Goldilocks. I can tell from the feel of those pearly white teeth."

Kate laughed, bent down to kiss him full on the lips, then sat down beside him. A waiter brought over menus. Tony tucked the newspaper under his chair and looked across at Kate.

"You look particularly vibrant," he said, studying her closely. "That means one of two things: Someone just offered you the key to the city, or you're trying real hard not to let me see how discouraged you feel."

"I'm not discouraged," she insisted.

"Where's the golden key?"

Kate sighed. "It's out there somewhere, waiting for me to claim it." She squeezed his hand. "I takes time to find a good job. We both know that I've only been on . . . a few interviews."

"Katie, I love you for trying so hard," he said softly, "but I want you to be honest with me. We have to be honest with each other or . . . or i isn't going to work."

"It's going to work," she said firmly. "Okay, I'm a little depressed. If you'd just spent an hour sit ting with a dour, red-faced guy like Harris Rob erts, you wouldn't be too happy, either. Worse, hi job offer matched his looks."

Tony leaned closer, kissing the tip of her nose "Sorry, Goldilocks."

She kissed him back, then picked up the menu "I'm going to drown my sorrows in a roast-bee special."

After they had both ordered, Kate bent down t reach for the newspaper. Tony caught her wrist "Don't read it now. You'll get indigestion befor you even get to eat your meal."

"That bad, huh?"

"I know a couple of realtors through Pete wh handle apartment rentals in the city. I made a appointment for two o'clock with one of them George Manchester. He's got a few places he ca show us today."

Kate nodded, trying not to think about he apartment back home. Not home for much longe she reminded herself. The thought did not do much to help her sinking spirits.

Their lunch over, Tony hailed a cab and they headed down to Manchester Realty. George Manchester was a very tall, very thin man with a shock of red hair and riveting blue eyes, eyes that traveled the length of Kate's body before he smiled broadly at both of them, saying he was sure he could find an apartment that would suit their needs.

"And our pocketbooks, I hope," Kate said sharply, pulling her blazer closed.

George Manchester showed them four apartments that day. They all had one thing in common: They were outrageously expensive. What was more depressing was the fact that not one of them seemed worth the price.

"Don't get discouraged," Manchester said, staring directly at Kate. "I can show you some other apartments tomorrow."

Tony drew her closer to his side, more than a little irritated at Manchester's seductive glances toward Kate. "We have other appointments for tomorrow." Ushering Kate to the door, he said curtly, "We'll get back to you."

"The creep," he muttered under his breath as they walked down the stairs, Tony too tense to wait for the elevator.

"Take it easy, Tony. It doesn't matter. We don't need to deal with someone like Manchester," she assured him, slipping her hand into his.

275

Tony's look was so bitter, she stopped short, pulling him to a halt at the landing. "What is it?"

He stared at her. "He reminded me up there of one of the . . . the guards at the prison. The way he kept looking at you, undressing you with his eyes, letting you know exactly what was on his mind."

"Tony, there are always men like that around."

"I know," he said dully, the image of that guard still sharply etched in his mind—and with it, the memories.

Kate put her arms around him. "Men like Manchester are not found only in prisons."

He forcibly shook the image from his mind smiling at her. "I know," he repeated, this time with more understanding. "Sorry, Kate. It still sneaks up on me at times. But I don't let it get me down anymore."

"I love you so much, Tony."

"Don't stop telling me that, Katie. Never stop." He took her in his arms, kissing her with such fervor that Kate was left breathless.

"Hey, come on. I refuse to fool around in one of Manchester's buildings." She grinned. "Let's get out of here."

They raced together down the rest of the stairs hand in hand, laughing, out of breath, resting hard against each other as they left the building. Two lovers on the lam. She shrugged off the thought telling herself she had to stop thinking of this move as running away with Tony. It would cast shadow over their relationship, shadows she wanted so desperately to dispel.

She was staying at the Gramercy Park Hotel for the week. They rode up in the elevator to her room, arms around each other, Tony stealing kisses as passengers came and went. They were both working hard at dispelling shadows, neither wanting to think about the flaws and problems in their plans. It was going to work. It had to work.

Tony scooped her up in his arms as she opened the door. "Just practicing." He grinned.

She locked her arms around his neck. "Practice makes perfect."

She pressed her lips against his rough cheek. He held her tighter, moving toward the bed, falling with her onto the carefully made covers.

For the rest of the afternoon they put depressing job interviews, dreary apartments, and ghosts aside. They clung to each other, holding on to the love that bound them together, the joy and wholeness they felt in being in each other's arms.

As the sun began to set they lay quietly, side by side. Tony turned his head toward Kate and studied her in profile. She smiled, feeling his gaze on her, but she didn't turn.

"What do you think?" she whispered. "Will I do?"

"Perfectly."

She laughed. "I always strive for perfection."

She turned to him then, her eyes meeting his,

her hand gently brushing the hair from his fore
head. "What are you thinking?" she whispered.

"Are you sure this is what you want?"

"I'm sure," she said quickly.

Too quickly, Tony thought.

Kate had promised Tony she'd hold off on hand
ing in her letter of resignation for a week after he
vacation. He insisted she give herself that time t
feel really sure she was doing the right thing. If sh
changed her mind, he would understand. Th
shuttle was still there. He'd do his best—they'
both do their best—to make time. . . .

Kate hated the thought of that shuttle. Sh
hated the thought of a relationship constantly sus
pended, airborne, never touching firm ground. Sh
needed to feel grounded. She wanted the kind c
commitment that required one of them to mak
the sacrifice.

Sacrifice. That was another thing she hated. Sh
shouldn't be viewing it that way.

She went to work each day, the letter of resigna
tion sitting in her briefcase. Every time she me
with Jud Howell, she felt like a traitor. Howell wa
the kind of boss you dream of finding—full c
praise, respect, and a purse string that wasn't for
ever tied in knots. In fact, she was due for a rais
in another three weeks. Instead she'd be leaving.

It was hardest dealing with Laura Gladston
Kate didn't want to tell her she was leaving befor

anding in her notice. It would put a burden on
Laura, to have to keep Kate's confidence.

Kate had a luncheon date with Laura for Tuesday afternoon. They met at Laura's favorite Chinese restaurant. Kate, having months earlier given
up ordering on her own when she was with Laura,
let her take care of the selections.

"You are going to love the Chef Yen Special
Chicken," Laura said, plucking her napkin off the
table and shaking it across her lap. "I was going to
order the Szechuan beef, but it's very spicy and
you've been looking kind of pale lately. I thought
your stomach might not be able to handle it."

Kate smiled. "You're probably right."

"That must have been some vacation last week."

"It was," she replied slowly, neatly unfolding
her napkin, primly adjusting it over her blue print
shirt.

Laura was smiling at her as Kate looked up. She
sighed, rubbing her hand wearily across her brow.
"I'm an open book, aren't I?"

Laura's smile broadened. "I can see some of the
writing, but not all of it."

"I'm leaving Howell and Beck, Laura. I wasn't
going to tell you until I'd handed in my notice. I
know this puts you in an awkward position, but I
don't want you to say anything until I give Jud my
letter of resignation on Friday. I was all set to do it
my first day back. Tony insisted I take the week"—
she paused, then went on—"and now I'm finding it harder and harder. I'm . . . I'm going to

279

miss this job. I went out on a few interviews i
New York." She made a face.

"That bad, huh?"

"Worse. It isn't even just the job market. Th
atmosphere, the pressure, the tension—the whol
feel of the scene in New York—turns me off. Sur
Howell and Beck is small potatoes compared t
some of the firms down there, but that's part o
what I like about it. I feel at home here. I gues
that's the biggest thing."

"Family's important," Laura said softly.

"There are all kinds of families. Lately the ide
of having one of my very own has become ver
appealing." Kate grinned. "I want my cake and
want to eat it too. Unfortunately they bake the on
I want only in New York."

"Tony won't consider moving back to Boston?

"I don't want him to, Laura. Not given the wa
he feels about it. As hard as my adjustment may t
to New York, it can't compare with the feelings h
would have to cope with here. No, it would t
worse for him. And worse for him is worse for us

"If you want my opinion—which you probab
can live without and which I plan to tell you an
way—I think it's a mistake," Laura said.

Kate held up her hand. "I know everythir
you're going to say. It isn't so much my not wan
ing to hear it. I've heard myself say everything o
the tip of your tongue too many times." Sh
looked evenly at Laura. "I'm going to do it an
way."

280

Laura nodded. "I can't say I wouldn't do the same thing in your situation."

Tony was packing up some books when Pete knocked on his bedroom door.

"Come on in."

"Packing already? The apartment isn't going to be ready for another couple of weeks."

"Just putting together a few things I won't be needing now."

Pete stretched out on the bed. "You sure about this apartment? I still think it's pretty pricy for what they're giving you."

Tony shrugged. "Nobody's giving anything away these days. You're in the business." He grinned. "You know the story. It's too bad I can't live in one of the office buildings we're leasing in town. Not that I could afford any of those, either."

"You deserve more than I can pay you, Tony. You're a real natural in the business. Don't get me wrong, you're an important asset to me, but I'm still too small to generate the kind of profits an established, wider-based firm brings in."

"Hey, I'm not complaining about the pay, am I? You not only gave me a job when I needed one badly, Pete, you opened up a whole new world for me. I love this business. The truth is, investment counseling wasn't ever for me. I can't count the number of nights I used to go home fighting off blinding tension headaches. The strain sometimes was unbearable." He gave his brother a wide grin.

"Hell of a way to discover that it was the wrong kind of work for me," he laughed.

Pete gave him a curious look. "You know, I think that's the first time I ever really heard you laugh like that about what happened."

Tony stopped short. "You're right. What do you know about that?"

"Maybe the demons are finally wearing out their welcome," Pete said, the humor gone from his tone.

Tony stared at him in surprise. "What's that supposed to mean?"

Pete sat up, leveling his eyes at his brother. "I mean that you may be holding on to them so that you have a valid excuse for . . . for hiding out." Before Tony could argue, Pete hurried on: "You're a free man, Tony, but you don't live like one."

"You and Kate have been talking."

"You're right. We both see what you're doing . . . and why. We also happen to understand and sympathize with you. Kate understands so deeply, she's willing to give up her career and her home for you."

Tony sank down onto the bed. "I keep thinking about that. She's the one making the sacrifices, taking the risks, giving up things that really matter to her because I'm . . . I'm a coward. I still wonder why the whole crazy mess happened to me? Why am I stuck having to carry the stigma around with me for the rest of my life?"

"Did you ever think that maybe the way to combat those thoughts is to try to live the rest of your life the way you want to?"

"The way I want to . . ." Tony echoed, his eyes going past his brother to a distant place coming slowly into clear focus.

The letter of resignation sat on the hall table next to her tan leather pocketbook. Tomorrow morning Kate would read it through one final time and hand it to Jud Howell. She tried out another speech in her mind: "I just want you to know what a valuable experience . . . what a meaningful experience . . . Working here has been such an important stepping-stone. . . ." No speech, she decided, dragging another carton filled with records across the room. Short and simple: "Thanks. I'm sorry I have to leave, but . . ."

Chris stopped by after work. Since their fiasco in Montreal, they had slowly gone back to being friends—less chummy, the seductive element effectively removed, but at least they hadn't blown it. Chris had been the first one she'd told that she was moving to New York. He was expecting it, clearly prepared to offer friendly support if not complete agreement that she was doing the right thing.

When she opened the door for him, he let out a low whistle. "Are you holding a bargain basement sale?"

"Very funny," she snapped, nearly tripping over a box of dishes.

"I thought you weren't leaving for three more weeks."

"I'm not, but I need to do something that makes this move feel real to me."

"Do you want some help?"

Kate gave him a weary smile. "No. Thanks, Chris, but I'm doing fine."

"Are you?"

"Don't you start."

"Okay. Okay. Just a last-minute try for an appeal."

"I thought we already gave each other pardons." She grinned.

Chris laughed, a slight flush on his otherwise rugged features. "Yeah, what am I thinking?"

Kate gave him an affectionate hug and steered him to the door. "I need to try to get some more work done."

"If you change your mind about anything, you know where to get ahold of me."

"Thanks, Chris. We'll definitely get together before I take off."

After he left, Kate sat down on the couch, staring bleakly around her. Her burst of energy was gone. She rested her chin on her hand and tried to think about what she ought to do next. She was still sitting there, thinking, when her downstairs buzzer went off. She sighed, not in the mood for more company tonight.

Tony's voice, sounding slightly fuzzy, came through the tinny speaker.

"What are you doing here?" Kate asked, incredulous.

"I didn't ride that shuttle in rush hour to tell you why from the lobby of your building."

Grinning, she buzzed him in and opened her front door to wait for him.

As the elevator came to a halt on her floor she had the fleeting thought that she probably looked a mess. From the look in Tony's eyes as he walked toward her, she saw that he wasn't in the least bit concerned about it.

"Hi, Goldilocks." He kissed her lightly, tenderly, then stepped inside. He came to an abrupt halt in the living room, stunned by the disarray. Kate walked past him and slumped down on the couch.

Tony laughed. "Aren't you the lady who once told me, 'A place for everything and everything in its place'?"

"I'm packing," she said irritably. Why did everyone think she was always working toward a girl-scout merit badge for neatness.

"How come?" Tony asked casually.

Kate stared up at him in disbelief. "What kind of a question is that?" she demanded. "And what are you doing here? It's only Thursday. Don't you have to work tomorrow? If you showed up to help me get my stuff together, forget it. I organize better on my own."

Tony sat down beside her. "You don't seem to be doing too well at this moment." His voice was soft, his fingers gently pressed around her arm. "Katie, is this what you want?"

"Tony, don't do this to me." There was pain in her voice. "I've tried everything else—the commuter bit, burying myself in my work, trying to keep you off my mind so I wouldn't go nuts. I even almost screwed up one of the best friendships I've ever had. I love you, and nothing else has worked. So I'm coming to New York. I'm going to find a job. I'm going to learn to love the apartment we found. I'm going to—"

He silenced her with a kiss. Then he held her at arm's length, his gaze warm and loving. "I've tried a lot of things, too, Kate. I didn't like the Sunday-night race to the airport any more than you did. Saying good-bye each time tore right into me. And the real estate business is terrific, but I can't take a signed lease to bed with me each night." He folded her into his arms, holding her fiercely, then he began to speak again, this time whispering against her silky hair. "Oh, Kate, it's taken such a long time for it to finally sink into this thick skull of mine that I don't have some invisible prison guard over my shoulder every step I take. I've been dragging him around with me without even realizing it. I don't have to escape over concrete walls; I need to knock down the ones I've erected myself. I haven't committed any crime." He said that with such vehemence, Kate was at last convinced he really had come to a new place.

"Kate"—he lifted her chin so their eyes met—"I

286

would be doing us both a terrible injustice if I allowed you to give up everything here to go into self-imposed exile with me."

"I'm willing to do that," she said, a small worried frown on her face. "I don't want to lose you, Tony."

He smiled. "Then sentence me to life . . . here with you."

She stared at him, the words slowly penetrating. "I'm . . . I'm a tough sentencer." She searched his face for a hint of doubt. "If I give you a life sentence, I'm going to throw away the key. No parole eligibility. We'll be stuck together for good," she warned, her heart leaping as he nodded confidently.

"Through sickness and in health; for better or for worse," he whispered, then held her tightly against him. "Oh, Katie, I love you, but I can't promise you a bed of roses. I still have those nightmares sometimes, and I don't know how long it's going to take me to finally get over—"

She pressed her lips to his for a long, loving kiss. "We've already been through the toughest times. And here we are, together in each other's arms. At least we won't have any more empty, lonely days . . . no more running away."

"When do I start serving my new sentence, Your Honor?" he murmured, slipping his hands over her breasts to the top button of her blouse, his lips moving to the tender hollow of her throat.

"Right now," she said with a soft moan as she let herself fall back across the couch. "So, start making the best of it."

"Exactly what I had in mind."